HARD LUCK JENNY

A HORROR NOVELLA

DAVID SODERGREN

Cover art by Cheryl Marriott

Paperback ISBN: 978-1-917910-06-4

For Heather

1

ASIDE FROM HIS NAME, THE THING DENNIS NORRIS HATED most about himself was his inability to go more than an hour without needing to pee.

The problem had begun in his late twenties, and only worsened over the ensuing decade, turning his and Mel's monthly theatre trips into gruelling tests of endurance as he fidgeted in his seat and counted down the minutes until the interval. Recently, he had even given up on the cinema, since the installation of new reclining chairs left little room to awkwardly squeeze past the other patrons' feet on his frequent visits to the bathroom.

But where his weak bladder was at its most bothersome was on the long drives between Edinburgh and Durness, a small village in the far north of Scotland his mother had inexplicably chosen to retire to. She claimed she wished to live near the sea, and when Dennis had pointed out her home town of Edinburgh was also by the sea, she had scoffed and sipped her wine and said, "Not *that* sea, dear."

He had no idea what she meant, but it was apparently a good enough reason for the obstinate battle-axe to move a six-hour drive away from her only kin and set up home in the most remote region of the country.

But Dennis was a good son, and despite the distance, he made the drive once a month to retune her telly and input her Wi-Fi password after she had somehow erased it from her computer for the umpteenth time. For her part, his mother prepared him delicious home-cooked meals, washed his socks, and tucked a hot water bottle into his bed like he was still a child and not a married man rapidly — *too* rapidly — approaching middle age.

Admittedly, it was not an unpleasant way to spend one weekend a month, but by Sunday, he longed for his freedom, and today was no exception. He had set off after a dinner — roast chicken with all the trimmings, followed by a bowl of ice cream with a Cadbury's Flake in it — and although he had only been driving an hour, already nature was calling. Normally, this would not have been an issue; Dennis *always* drove the same carefully planned route, one which ensured he was never far from a public toilet or motorway service station. But shortly after leaving Durness, an unexpected problem had presented itself.

A fallen tree on the road had sent him on a baffling diversion into uncharted territory, and in the fifty minutes since, he had driven alongside an old logging trail through miles of thick woodland, with nary a town or village in sight. If he didn't come across one soon, he'd—

"*Are you listening to me?*" Mel asked over the phone.

"Yeah, sorry," he chuckled, glad his wife was keeping him company on the drive. "I just really need to pee."

"*Well, there's a shock.*" He could practically *hear* her eyes rolling. "*Where are you now?*"

"I'm not sure. Middle of nowhere. All I can see are trees."

"*Then pull over and go in the woods. No one's gonna see you.*"

She was right, of course. Since setting off, he hadn't passed a single vehicle on the deserted roads. And what did he care if anyone saw him peeing by the side of the road, anyway?

Well, for a start, public urination is illegal, and—

"You still there?"

"Huh? Yeah, sorry. I was thinking."

"Well, try not to drift off. Those roads are dangerous."

He detected a note of caution in Mel's voice. Understandable... but unnecessary. He had already survived one car wreck, and would never make the same mistake again. After the accident, it had taken him a full year to get back behind the wheel, and even now he navigated the roads with the nervous vigilance of a learner driver.

Of course, he wasn't drunk this time, which helped.

Don't think about it.

How could he not? Last Tuesday had been the two-year anniversary of his newfound sobriety, a landmark he celebrated with a Domino's pepperoni pizza and a can of full-fat Coke all to himself. He hadn't touched a drop of booze since that fateful day, and he intended to keep it that way.

Still, he supposed Mel was right to worry. The sun had vanished behind the impossibly tall trees, and the narrow, winding country roads were slick with rain.

Welcome to northern Scotland, he thought grimly. *Come for the shite weather, stay for the, uhh, shite weather.*

The speedometer nudged forty, and he eased off the pedal as he approached a bend. Through the windshield, slivers of light flickered between the trees.

"Hey, wait a minute. I see something."

"What?"

Rainwater pounded against the windscreen as he took the corner doing a little over thirty, his wipers glancing across the glass with a series of excruciating squeaks. The road straightened before him, and he squinted into the darkness.

"Come on, come on," he muttered.

Ahead, the trees seemed to fall away on both sides. On the left was nothing but the vast emptiness of a field. But to his right...

"Well?" asked Mel, her voice crackling through the speaker.

"I see buildings."

"What? I can't hear you."

"I see buildings," he half-shouted. He didn't want to get his hopes up and risk tricking his bladder into relaxing, but it appeared to be a collection of small crofts and larger two-storey cottages.

"That's promising," said Mel.

"I'm not so sure. It looks pretty dead."

Each building lurked in the shadows with their curtains drawn, as if the occupants had already turned in for the night. A solitary streetlamp provided scant illumination, lighting one small section of pavement and a red post box. Was that the light he'd seen through the trees? Dennis's hope evaporated. With each passing second, his chances of finding somewhere to pee dwindled. Soon, he'd have to—

Wait.

Was that...?

"Yes!" he cried, pumping his fist in victory before quickly placing his hand back on the steering wheel. He smiled to himself as warm, golden light flooded onto the wet road from a wide building tucked behind a bank of pine trees. He subconsciously sped up, flexing his thigh muscles in antic-ipation.

"Is it a town?" asked Mel.

"Almost. More of a village." He sighed. "Thank heavens for that."

"Thank heavens indeed," Mel replied, her teasing sarcasm not lost on him. *"Is there somewhere you can go? A hotel, or—"*

"No hotel," he said. "Just..." His mouth felt dry, and he cleared his throat. "Just a pub."

"Oh." Mel's disappointment was palpable. She had never been adept at hiding her feelings.

"I can keep driving. There's bound to be another town soon, or a petrol station—"

"No, don't be silly. If you gotta go..."

"You gotta go," he finished, as he pulled the Toyota up alongside the stone building and killed the engine. There he waited, the car silent except for heavy raindrops drumming off the roof. "I won't be long, babe."

"I know."

"Just gonna nip in, do my business, and come straight back." He hesitated. "You can stay on the line if you like."

She was quiet. Too quiet, as if seriously contemplating his suggestion. Then, she said, *"No, that's silly. I'm sorry. I do trust you. You know that, right?"*

"I do."

"Good. So quit your yapping and go pee, and call me when you're back on the road."

"I will," he smiled. "Okay, better go. The Rockarn Inn is calling me."

"Rockarn? Sounds like a metal bar."

"Maybe." He glanced out the rain-smeared window. "But it sure as hell doesn't look like one. Talk to you soon."

"Enjoy your pee. Love you!"

"Love you." He hung up, and steeled himself. Mel needn't worry about him getting drunk, not anymore. The accident had instilled in him an almost Pavlovian response to alcohol. Nowadays, the smell of it — even the *idea* of it — made him nauseous. He hated going into pubs, and actively avoided work nights out due to his newfound phobia, but today, circumstances dictated he must face his fear head-on.

Leaving the security of his car, he stepped into the torrential downpour. With its gabled roof and harled walls, the pub looked like it had been standing since the Reformation. The voices of several men bellowing a raucous folk song bled out, while dark shapes bounded and spun past the welcoming glow of the windows.

"Sounds lively," he mumbled, and wondered whether his bladder could possibly hold on a wee while longer. There was nothing worse than walking into a bustling pub, especially a rural one where everybody undoubtedly knew each other and outsiders were frowned upon. Even back when he had been an alcoholic, the act of sheepishly entering an unfamiliar pub always reminded him of the opening scene of *An American Werewolf in London*. But dammit, he was *desperate,* so he buried his inhibitions and jogged through the rain. Under the fabric awning, Dennis took a breath and pushed the door open. A bell jangled metallically above him, but few turned to look at the interloper.

Jeez, the place was *rammed*.

It must have been a special occasion. Or perhaps — and this seemed the more likely option — there was nothing else to do in Rockarn on a Sunday night. Regardless, it appeared the entire village was crammed into every available nook and cranny. People jostled by the bar, breaking out in raucous laughter. Others danced to the folk music, waving pint glasses back and forth, the beer frothing over the sides and spilling down their shirts and jackets. Beyond them was a snooker table, around which several men and women crowded.

Terrific.

Wishing to get the ordeal over with, Dennis shuffled between the cramped bodies, contorting himself into bizarre shapes to avoid bumping into anyone. "Excuse me," he muttered as he passed each person. "Thanks... ta... cheers."

The pub was surely over capacity. And where were the loos? He couldn't see anything through the assembled throng, and felt like a dad who had agreed to take his daughter to a Taylor Swift concert and somehow ended up caught in the middle of the crowd. But while he couldn't find the toilet, he *was* in sight of the bar. Squeezing between two burly men in Shetland jumpers, he sidled up to the counter and signalled to the barman, who promptly turned away.

Mustn't have seen me, thought Dennis, though he had trouble believing it.

As he waited patiently, a pretty young woman at the far end of the bar caught his attention. She dabbed at her glassy eyes with a handkerchief as several older women fussed around her. Dennis removed his glasses, wiped the rain from the lenses with his sleeve, and looked again.

Yup. The young woman was *definitely* wearing a ram's skull on her head, balanced atop a crown of dead flowers.

"*What'll it be, then?*"

Dennis looked up at the barman in surprise. "Huh?"

"I said, what'll it be, son?"

"Oh, uh, a Coke, thanks." He had no intention of drinking the beverage — more liquid at this stage would be a foolish move indeed — but he also knew from experience he'd have to buy a drink to use the facilities. In his current state, it was a battle he was unwilling to fight.

The barman glared at him. "A Coke?" He shook his head in what appeared to be disgust. "On a bloody night like this..." He half-filled a glass and slammed it down in front of Dennis. "Four pounds."

"Four?" He considered mentioning that the sign behind the bar listed a vodka and Coke for one pound fifty, but right now, Dennis didn't care. His leg twitched as he fished a fiver from his wallet and handed it to the barman. "Where are the toilets?" The man jerked a thumb towards the back of the room and walked away.

Dennis waited for his change, but the surly bugger never returned. This was going to be the most expensive piss of his life. "Rude," he grumbled, and stole a final glance at the crying woman in the skull headwear.

So weird.

He figured it must be some old folk custom, then abandoned his Coke and snaked through the crowd.

The pub was, in its own way, charmingly retro. There were hipster bars back in Edinburgh that would give their ironic stuffed deer heads for a fraction of the rough-hewn, rustic charm on display. From the wood-panelled walls and chipped mirror to the well-loved dartboard and threadbare carpet, the vibes — as the young folk Dennis taught liked to say — were unreal.

Three doors lined the far wall, and as Dennis neared, he looked back at the bar, and at the woman still sobbing while her entourage comforted her. She leaned forward, resting her head on her hands, and only then did he notice the black veil tucked behind her hair.

"Oh, shoot."

Suddenly, the curiously busy pub made a whole heap

more sense. Glancing at the occupants, he saw more veils, more black dresses, and men in smart, dark suits.

"You idiot," he whispered, and bit his lip.

He had stumbled into someone's *wake*.

Okay. That was no problem. He wasn't staying, not when he had the best part of a five-hour drive — or longer, depending on the diversion — ahead of him. Ideally, he could slip in and out without being noticed, and luckily, so far only the grumpy barman had paid him any attention. He entered the bathroom — dammit, the only cubicle was in use — and unbuckled his belt by the urinal. There, he closed his eyes and emptied his bladder, relishing the sweet release.

A toilet flushed behind him, followed by the clunky rattle of a lock. As his urine arced against the filthy ceramic, someone left the cubicle and washed their hands in the sink.

Please don't talk to me, please don't talk to me, please don't—

"A sad day," the man said in a gruff voice. "You gonnae miss him, aye?"

Dennis kept his head down.

"Ah said, you gonnae miss him?"

Hot damn, could he not piss in peace? He turned his head towards the man, who was wiping his wet hands on his trousers. An older gentleman, he wore a dusty black suit and a belligerent look on his weather-beaten face.

"Oh, uh, sorry," said Dennis. "I don't actually know, umm... the deceased."

The man continued wiping his hands, his steely gaze never wavering. "You didnae ken Colin?"

Dennis kept peeing. He wished he could stop, and also that the man would quit staring at him. "Is, uh, Colin the..." — *how the hell to word it?* — "...is this Colin's wake?"

"Aye, it's fucking *Colin's wake,* you wee cunt." The man stepped closer. "And I dinnae think yer very funny."

Dennis could smell the man's aftershave. He glanced down at the urinal, where his stream was mercifully coming to an end. A few seconds, he told himself, and he'd be back on the road.

"I'm not trying to be funny," he said, unused to holding a conversation while peeing. "I... I just stopped to use the bathroom. I'm on my way home from Durness, you see, and—"

"Lucky you," the man snapped. "But poor Colin's never goin' home again, is he?"

A heavy silence filled the room. Was it a rhetorical question? The man didn't move, and Dennis thought he'd better answer. "No, I guess he's not."

"Because he's *dead.*"

Dennis tucked himself into his trousers and fastened his belt. "Yeah. It's tragic." He moved to use the sink, but the man blocked his path.

"You should pay yer respects tae Jenny," he said.

Dennis offered him a tired smile. "I don't know who that is."

"Colin's widow, ya wee gobshite. You should pay yer respects."

Dennis didn't like the man's tone, but he also didn't like the man's thick, brawny arms and cold, psychotic stare.

"I would," he said, "but honestly, I've never met—"

"She's had a rough year."

"I can imagine."

"The fuck you can." The man took another step closer.

Dennis motioned towards the sink. "Uh, may I use..."

He refused to budge, instead repeating, "You should pay yer respects tae Jenny."

"I will," said Dennis, his voice dripping with forced sincerity. "I will *definitely* do that. I'm sorry."

"Disrespectful bastard," the man snorted, and shoved Dennis against the cubicle before storming out of the bathroom.

The door swung shut, and he was alone once more, his heart hammering in his chest.

"Guess I'll go pay my respects then," he said, in a voice so quiet he barely heard it himself. "You freaking weirdo."

2

WITH A LONG SIGH — AND A PRICKLE OF HUMILIATION — Dennis fastidiously washed his hands. The encounter had rattled him, but he felt better having peed, and looked forward to hitting the road. Time was ticking on, and he had to be at school eight-fifteen Monday morning for the staff meeting. At this rate, he'd be lucky if he got more than six hours of sleep.

He turned off the tap and reached for the paper towel dispenser. It was empty.

"Savages," he muttered, and wiped his hands on his corduroy trousers before exiting the bathroom.

The wake was, regrettably, in full swing.

On a low stage, a man perched atop a stool with an acoustic guitar on his lap, strumming a lively — and distinctly ribald — tune. Thanks to the rowdy group of hollering drunkards, Dennis struggled to discern the lyrics, but they appeared to refer to a woman of ill repute. He noticed it was all men singing along, and shook his head.

Good to know misogyny's alive and well in the countryside, he thought wryly, and made his way through the crowd.

Sweat and alcohol fumes mingled into an overpowering stench, and he had to peel the soles of his shoes up from the stained carpet. All the while, he watched for the man who had accosted him in the bathroom.

Don't worry about him, he told himself. *He was obviously drunk and upset. You should have been a good sport and played along.*

True, true. Would it have killed him to pretend to know the deceased? At least then he could have avoided an uncomfortable confrontation.

As he passed the bar, he glanced at the woman with the ram's skull on her head. Jenny, presumably. She was still crying. Should he pay his respects to her as promised? Ah, but what the hell would he say? He didn't know the woman, and he certainly didn't know poor old dead Colin. His words would come from a place of insincerity, and honestly, wasn't that worse than saying nothing at all?

She looked up at him, and their eyes met. He realised he had been staring.

Damn.

He had broken his cardinal rule: to avoid conversation, *never* make eye contact. Squeezing between two jocular men, he lowered his head and quickened his pace, making a break for the door. He was almost there when a hand gripped his arm, pulling him back.

"Goin' somewhere, pal?"

He turned towards a half-man, half-tank with a bald head and a face that looked like a caricature brought to life by dark sorcery. The ruddy-cheeked brute towered over him by a good six inches.

"Just heading home." Dennis offered him a false smile. "Got a long drive ahead of me."

The man released him and rested his enormous paw on

the door, preventing Dennis from opening it. "You're no' fae around here, are ya?"

Why was everyone suddenly so interested in him? He supposed they didn't get many visitors in this far-flung neck of the woods, and it was natural to be curious. Maybe this chap was being friendly?

"No," said Dennis. He chuckled. "I'm from Edinburgh, actually. I only stopped to use the bathroom."

"Edinburgh, aye?" A quizzical expression darkened the man's face. "Never heard of it."

Dennis tried to gauge his seriousness. "Edinburgh," he said, more forcefully this time. The man stared blankly at him. "Our capital city? Where the Scottish parliament is?"

Nothing. Not a flicker of recognition.

He kept trying. "Edinburgh Castle? The festival?"

"The harvest festival? Nah, mate, that's in Fat Henry's field."

"What? No, I mean the arts and culture... look, it doesn't matter. I really have to go. Got work in the morning. Back to the daily grind, y'know?"

The man kept his weight resting against the door. "So that's it, then? You're just gonnae fuck off, aye?"

Was that a threat or a genuine question?

"Yes?" Dennis replied, unsure of himself. "It... it was nice meeting you all?"

"It's Colin's wake."

Dennis nodded. What did the brute want from him? "I don't know Colin. I told you, I'm not from around here. I only stopped to—"

The veins on the man's neck bulged. "It's Colin's fucking *wake*."

"Yeah, I *know* that, but—"

"So you *do* know Colin?" His eyes narrowed. "Have you been lyin' tae me?"

Flustered, Dennis took a moment to think. "No," he said carefully. "I stopped to use the bathroom, that's all." His throat grew tighter. "While I was in there, someone told me it was Colin's wake. If I'd known this was a private function, I would never have intruded. I'm very sorry."

The scowl dropped from the man's face, replaced by a cautious smile. "Aye, awright then. Come on, I'll buy you a drink."

For the first time since arriving, the gnawing dread in Dennis's stomach dissipated. Not entirely, of course. But a little. He had handled himself well in the face of unbridled aggression, and took the time to mentally congratulate himself for defusing the situation. "Thank you, that's very kind, but I have to be off." He yanked on the door handle, but the man kept it firmly shut.

"Just one." The man's smile looked more pained than before. "Jenny's lost her husband," he said, as if a stranger's loss was reason enough to postpone a five-hour journey through the rainy, treacherous night.

"I'm aware of that," said Dennis. "But I don't *know* Jenny, just like I don't know Colin. I don't know *anyone* here, because I don't *live* here. I told you, I'm just passing through on my way home to Edinburgh."

The man mulled this information over, and ignored it. "One drink. Show some compassion. One wee drink... for our sweet Jenny."

"Did you not hear me?" Dennis tried to maintain his composure. "I don't know her, okay? I'm sorry for her loss, I really am, but I have a long drive, and I'd like to get home before—"

Dennis gasped as the man's huge hand shot between his legs, the chunky fingers tightening around his penis and testicles.

"Dinnae raise your voice at me, you speccy shite." He gripped harder, and Dennis let out an involuntary wheeze. "You might not give a fuck about Jenny, but the folks in this village do. We look after our own here. Always have, always will."

"Okay," Dennis panted, his balls grinding together.

"She's a right wee doll, that one. But her luck's no' in at the moment."

"Okay, okay. Please, let me—"

"So stay fae a drink. Maybe even two." The fist tightened. "You might even enjoy our company."

Dennis was *not* enjoying the vice-like pressure on his balls, but he nodded eagerly until the man relinquished his grip. With tears in his eyes, and his junk throbbing in his underpants, he turned away and waddled towards the bar, ashamed of the way the man had so easily emasculated him. Thank goodness no one had seen.

Well, as far as he knew.

He reached the bar and leaned against the wooden counter, wiping tears from his eyes. His cock pulsed, and his stomach churned. How long would he have to stay before it was reasonable to leave? They couldn't keep him here, dammit! He was a grown man who was simply in the wrong place at the wrong time.

His Coke was where he had left it, so he picked up the cool glass and wet his parched throat.

Great. Now you'll need to pee again in half an hour.

In his periphery, the woman watched him.

Jenny.

Go to her. Say something.

But what? What are you supposed to say to a stranger in a situation like this?

How about, I'm sorry for your loss?

Would that be enough? Why would she even care what he had to say? Blast it, they didn't *know* each other!

He took another drink and glanced around the room, looking anywhere but at Jenny. Floral garlands drooped from the walls, the dried flowers black and withered. Below them hung a single framed photo of a man with his eyes closed. It was a strange choice of image, but not half as strange as the scrawled writing beneath it.

COLIN

HE HAD HIS TIME

LET OTHERS RISE UP AND FIGHT

Dennis scratched his chin. These people were nuts. How long would he be stuck here with them? Mel would be wondering why he hadn't called. He checked his pockets for his phone, finding only his keys and his wallet. A shiver of panic ensued, until he remembered it was still in the car.

"Excuse me," he said to the barman. "Do you happen to have the time?"

The man glared at him. "Sorry, son, are we keeping you?"

"I only asked—"

"You got somewhere better to be?"

"As a matter of fact, yes," said Dennis. "I'm *trying* to get home."

The barman regarded him contemptuously. "Jenny's lost her husband. Don't you care?"

"Honestly, no, I..." He quickly stopped himself before he said something he'd regret. "I mean, of *course* I care. But I'm not supposed to be here, and all I want is—"

Someone tapped him on the shoulder. Christ, what now? Warily, he turned, coming face-to-face with the dark, abyssal eye-sockets of a skull. Beneath the weathered bone and cracked, rotten teeth, a woman regarded him with bloodshot eyes, her face streaked with tears.

Jenny.

"Oh," he said.

Quick, pay your respects.

"You must be—"

She struck him across the cheek with a powerful slap. The impact rocked his head to the side, the stinging *whack* resounding throughout the bar.

Twang!

The musician strummed a duff chord as one of the guitar strings snapped. Speechless, Dennis touched a hand to his cheek. The room fell silent. *Horrendously* silent.

"I'm sorry my husband's death has inconvenienced you," Jenny said, loud enough for everyone to hear. Then she burst into tears, as two women clad head-to-toe in black rushed to her side and ushered her away. As they did so, one turned to Dennis and hissed at him like a threatened cat.

He felt the revellers' eyes upon him.

Do something. Say something, you idiot!

"I'm sorry," he called after her.

Is that it?

Yes, it was. He could think of *nothing* to say that would improve his situation. Clearly, it was his cue to leave before some grieving nutter smashed his face in. Leaving his Coke on the counter for the second time, he turned from the bar and—

The shaven gorilla from the door blocked his path. The man's neck was somehow wider than his head. "You've upset Jenny, ya cunt," he said, his hand — the one that had gripped Dennis by the balls — flexing repeatedly.

"I... I didn't mean to. It's all been a misunderstanding."

"Jenny lost her *husband*."

Yeah, so everyone keeps telling me, Dennis considered saying. But wishing to keep his teeth in his mouth, he instead apologised again. "I said I'm sorry. What more do you want from me?"

"Sorry's no' good enough." He grabbed Dennis's collar and wrenched him close. "So how about we step outside and settle this like men? The winner gets—"

"Och, leave the wee laddie alone, Roddy!"

The thug released Dennis and raised his arms as if under arrest. He stepped away, although his ruthless gaze never wavered. Dennis fixed his collar with trembling hands as the man retreated. His rescuer — an elderly woman in a black dress, her friendly face lined with wrinkles — patted his arm.

"Here, come sit with me a minute," she said, and tugged on his sleeve. "I'm sure we can straighten this nasty business out."

With his cheek still stinging from Jenny's slap, and the rest of his face burning with embarrassment, Dennis followed as she led him to a table in the corner. Through the window, he saw his Toyota parked outside in the rain. The sight of it almost made him cry. Only a thin pane of glass separated him from his ride out of this godforsaken village, yet for all his attempts to leave, the car may as well have been a mile away.

The woman gestured for him to sit, and this time he decided to play along.

"Thank you," he said, and perched on a wooden chair with one leg shorter than the others. The pub was awash with furtive murmurs, but all it took was the single crack of one snooker ball against another for normal service to resume. The musician had restrung his guitar and began to play, and in a heartbeat, people were up and dancing and making merry.

Glad to no longer be the centre of attention, Dennis fiddled with his wedding ring and looked at the woman. She watched him keenly over the rims of her glasses, saying nothing. He had the strange feeling he was being tested.

"I guess everyone's quite emotional tonight," he said.

"Aye, that they are." She put her hand on his, and it took all of Dennis's willpower not to flinch away from her touch. He was no fan of physical contact with strangers, but he did not wish to appear ungrateful. She sighed. "That they are."

"Yeah," said Dennis. He glanced around the pub.

The woman patted his hand. "Aye." She smiled wistfully, and repeated herself a third time. *"That they are."*

Dennis nodded. It was the most boring conversation of his life. "Well," he said, and started to rise from his chair. "I think it's time for me to—"

"What's your name, love?" she interrupted.

"Dennis." Wearily, he sat back down. This was not going to be as easy as he'd hoped. "My name is Dennis."

"Dennis. What a pretty name. Little Darling Dennis."

He forced a chuckle, secretly plotting his escape route through the crowd.

"My name, not that you've asked, is Mrs Roberta Flowers, and I apologise for the behaviour of that reprobate at the bar. Our Roddy thinks that because he delivers our letters, he's part of everybody's business."

"Oh, it's fine. We got our wires crossed, that's all. See, I was just passing through, and—"

"Poor Jenny," Roberta said. She glanced at the crying woman. "So awful, losing another husband like that."

"*Another* husband?"

"Aye. It's a difficult time for our wee community. Colin's the third one she's lost this year."

"The *third?*"

"We're all a little shaken up by it."

Dennis raised his eyebrows. "I'll say. It's only June."

The woman smiled understandingly, as if — in her deranged mind — what she was saying was normal. "Aye, poor Jenny. Hard Luck Jenny, some folks around here call her."

Sounds appropriate, Dennis thought, and sat forwards, leaning his elbows on the table. "Now, when you say she 'lost' three husbands, do you mean...?" He waited for her to fill in the blanks, but she only gawped at him dumbly. "Like, did they all die?"

"Well, I don't mean she *misplaced* them," Roberta replied curtly. "She didn't lose three husbands down the back of the settee."

"No, no, I didn't mean that."

"So what *did* you mean?" Her smile faded. "You wouldn't be making fun of us, would you, Little Darling Dennis?"

"Absolutely not," he said. He would wait until he got in the car and called Mel before doing that. "I'm trying to understand the timeline, that's all. Were they married at... y'know, the same time?"

"Of course not. We may be old-fashioned, but we no longer practice bigamy." The chair creaked as Roberta leaned back. "Aye, poor old Jenny. All she wants is to settle down and start a family. Isn't she a wee smasher?"

It was Dennis's turn to smile. He did so, and Roberta stared at him. Did she want an answer? Was she honestly expecting him to comment on the attractiveness of a woman grieving the death of her husband?

Her third in six months, he reminded himself.

"Yeah," he said noncommittally. "She's a real knockout." At least that wasn't a lie. Behind the tears and the grief, the woman was indeed rather good-looking. If he was half his age, he might have fancied the pants off her. But as a thirty-nine-year-old, the glow of youth no longer held the same appeal it once had. What he appreciated in his wife was her companionship, her sense of humour, and her creativity. Oh, and her big tits, naturally. He *was* still a red-blooded male at heart.

"A real knockout, eh?" Roberta said. "Well, I'm glad you think so."

"Oh? Why's that?" He immediately regretted asking.

Under the table, Roberta's foot grazed his leg. She lowered her voice, and, with a sly wink, said, "Some folks say she gets her looks from her mother."

Even for Dennis, who was no expert at body language, it was hard to miss the implication. Was this Jenny's mother? She couldn't be. She was too old. At a conservative guess, this woman was in her eighties, while Jenny could be no older than twenty—

The woman's foot found his ankle. She must have removed her shoe, because her ragged toenails scratched across his shin and tugged his sock down.

"Do you want to know why Jenny's the best shag in the village?" she rasped.

Dennis tucked his legs under the chair. "No, thank you."

"It's because," Roberta said, licking her chapped lips, "I taught her everything she knows."

Dennis stared at her. Words deserted him.

"If you get a chance," the old woman continued, "give her taint a wee tickle. Lick it, even. She loves when men—"

"I'm gonna get some air," said Dennis, rising too fast and bumping his knee against the table. "It was, um, a pleasure talking with you, uh..."

"Mrs Roberta Flowers," she said, her leering eyes focused on his crotch.

"That's right. Roberta. Of course."

"There's a garden out back you can use. They won't let you out the front. Not yet. You've not paid your respects to—"

He walked away, leaving her gums flapping.

Give her taint a wee tickle.

In all his years of teaching teenagers, Dennis had never heard anything quite so inappropriate as a widow's mother offering vulgar sex tips for her grieving daughter.

Lick it.

It wasn't just inappropriate... it was outrageous. He couldn't stay here a second longer, yet when he approached the main door, the brute from earlier eyeballed him menacingly.

Dennis halted, scratched his head thoughtfully as if remembering something important, and walked in the opposite direction, taking a wide berth around the dance floor. Cool air filtered in through a back door, and he headed for it. Pinned to the wood was a handwritten sign that read KEEP THE NOISE DOWN - NO SPILLING OF BLOOD ON THE PREMISES. He yanked the door open and stepped into the rain.

The garden consisted of a couple of picnic benches set into concrete, each with its own oversized red-and-white umbrella. A few potted plants dotted the area, the flora inside them long-dead, the soil stuffed with cigarette butts. It felt good to be outside, but Dennis's initial joy gave way to despair at the high brick wall that surrounded the garden. Sharp stones and wicked shards of broken glass had been cemented into the top layer, and covered with coils of barbed wire. The walls resembled those of a Russian gulag rather than a country pub.

He wandered the perimeter, searching for a foothold, or a section of barbed wire that looked thinner and less deadly than the rest.

Nothing.

There was no escape.

Still, at least, out here, he could recharge. The rain soothed his skin, almost like he had woken from a nightmare drenched in cold sweat. Perhaps, if he remained in the garden long enough, everyone would be so drunk by the time he came back that they wouldn't notice him leaving?

A pipe dream... but for now, it would have to suffice.

He sat on a bench. The wet seat soaked his corduroys, but he didn't care. A dog barked in the distance, and a phone rang.

His phone.

The ringtone he had chosen for Mel was the Imperial March from *The Empire Strikes Back,* a private joke between the pair of them due to the black cape she had worn on an early date. On the other side of the wall, the muffled orchestral theme screeched tinnily from inside his car. Jesus. He wondered how many missed calls he'd have. She'd probably think he was drunk and lying in a pool of his own vomit.

"Goddammit," he said, and hit his fist off the table. This was ridiculous. Absolutely *ridiculous*. They couldn't hold him here. Who the hell did these mad bastards think they were?

"I'm going home," he muttered, and strode towards the door, his feet splashing in shallow puddles... and there she was, standing in the doorway.

The woman.

The widow.

The one they called... Hard Luck Jenny.

3

———————

"HEY," SAID JENNY, PEERING AT HIM FROM BENEATH THE RAM'S skull. Up close, he noticed it was attached to the dead flower crown by black satin ribbons knotted beneath her chin. "Can we talk?"

I don't want to, I don't want to, I don't want to, I don't—

"Sure," said Dennis. "Of course we can. You wanna go inside? It's raining."

She touched his hand, her fingers delicately brushing his skin. "No. Out here is fine." Her grip tightened, and she led him just like her mother had done. Why did everyone keep touching him?

"I'm sorry for earlier," she said as they strolled in a slow circle around the garden. The rain battered the skull and pooled in the empty eye sockets. "I don't know what came over me."

"It's no problem, honestly. I was being obnoxious."

"No, it's not your fault." She looked at her feet, and the rainwater spilled out of the sockets like floods of tears. "I'm upset, that's all. And while I'm glad everyone is looking out for me, sometimes I just want to be left alone, y'know?"

Dennis did know. For a start, he wished she'd let go of his hand and leave *him* alone. But this was a promising development. If he could make amends with Jenny and somehow get into her good graces, he might actually be allowed to go home.

"I understand," he smiled. "And I'm really very sorry for your loss."

"Colin was special. I'm going to miss him."

He gave her fragile hand a tiny squeeze, and managed to pull away from her. "He will certainly be missed," he said with a knowing nod.

She raised her head to look up at him, and he could understand why some men would find her irresistible. Hypnotic green eyes glistened within her porcelain face, her red lips slightly parted.

"Thank you for saying that," she said, and Dennis flinched in surprise as she wrapped her arms around him and buried her face in his chest. The sharp snout of the skull dug awkwardly into his collarbone. "And thank you for coming. I'm so glad one of his close friends could make it."

Dennis stood stock-still. "Pardon?"

"Not one person from outside the village came to the wake. Not a single soul." Her voice vibrated his chest as every curve of her body pressed against his. "Except for you."

Oh.

She took his head in both hands and pulled him close, kissing him once on his left cheek, and once on his right.

Oh no.

"Thank you," she said, and kissed him on the lips. "Colin would be so happy to know you came."

Oh no no no.

She thought he was an old friend of her dead husband?

27

No, this will not do. This will not do at all.

"Uh, listen," he said, wriggling free of her grasp. "I didn't... I mean, I'm not—"

She clung onto him again, enormous sobs wracking her body. "It's been so hard. I thought that maybe my life with Colin had been a lie. That he hadn't told his friends about us, or his family. I started to question everything."

Dennis inhaled through his teeth. "Yeah, see, the thing is—"

"I wanted to die," she wept. "I really did. I even considered suicide to free myself from the torment. Last night, I sat naked in my bathtub and held a razor to my wrists, daring myself to... ah, but now, talking to you, his old friend..." With what looked like great effort, she gazed into his eyes, her lipstick smeared across her mouth. "...it's like he's still here with me."

Ah, bollocks.

What the hell was he supposed to say to that? This ghoulish charade had to end. He was no friend of Colin, a man he had never even heard of until fifteen bloody minutes ago. And yet... what harm would it do to pretend, if it made the woman feel better about herself? If it made her want to *live?*

She placed his hand on her left breast. "My heart. Can you feel it?"

Dennis felt several things; apprehension, terror, the lace of her bra. He tried to remove his hand, but she wouldn't let him.

"Can you *feel* it?" she asked emphatically. "Can you feel my heart beating with joy?"

He cleared his throat. "Uh, I can feel something, all right."

"That's because of *you*. Without you, this heart might no longer beat."

Right, that's enough. Put a stop to this nonsense before it goes—

"Well," he shrugged, "it's the least I could do for my dear friend Colin."

Oh boy.

Jenny wiped away a tear. "It's what he would have wanted, isn't it?"

"Sure," said Dennis, though as he removed his hand from Colin's wife's tit, he doubted this was any dead man's last wish. Tucking his hands safely in his pockets, he looked past Jenny to the doorway, where a muscular man with a face like a smacked arse glared at him, his fists hardening into two slabs of granite.

Unaware of his presence, Jenny laughed. "I'm sorry. Here I am opening my heart to you, and I don't even know your name."

"Dennis." He offered his hand, and she shook it. "Pleased to meet you."

"I'm Jenny. But you already knew that, didn't you?"

"Sure did. Colin spoke about you often."

What are you doing? What are you saying?

It was a big mistake, but when he saw the smile that lit up her face, he knew he'd done the right thing. "Come on," he said. "Let's go back—"

"How did you know him?"

Dennis froze. Did she suspect something? Was this a freakin' test all of a sudden? Seconds passed like days.

Better answer her.

He looked at her pretty face, then at the intense scowl of the brute in the doorway.

"School," he said.

Idiot! You don't know how old he was!

Damn, that was true.

Quick, fix it. Fix the lie!

"We went to school together," he clarified. "High school."

You've made it worse!

"Oh!" Her eyes widened. "You went to school in Italy too?"

A sinking feeling opened in Dennis's gut. "Italy? Yes. Yes, I did." He paused, trying to think of any Italian words. "Sì."

"Che carino!" She grabbed his arm, a wide smile beaming across her face. "Sono felice di conoscerti. Come stai?"

He stared at her blankly. What the hell had she just said?

An uneasy silence filled the air.

"I'm sorry," said Jenny, her cheeks colouring. "My Italian was never any good. I've made a fool of myself, haven't I?"

"No, no, it was perfect. I'm rusty, that's all. But I understood every word."

If his internal monologue could sigh, it would have done so.

"Really? You understood me?"

Come on, then. Say something, you idiot. Speak Italian — a language you do not know — to her.

"Sì," he said again, and smiled weakly. Out of sheer desperation, he touched a finger to the tip of her nose, and said, "Le boop!"

For the longest time, she stared at him, seemingly out of bewilderment. Then she smiled. Soon, the smile turned into melodic laughter so infectious that Dennis found himself joining in.

God, he had to get out of here.

"Le boop," she said, shaking her head. "That's *French.*" She pressed his nose with her own finger, letting it linger a little too long. "Le boop to *you,* funny guy."

The brute in the doorway inched closer. "Right, Jenny," he said. "It's time fae the speeches."

"Oh. Of course. Thank you, Nigel." She turned to leave, then hesitated. "I hope we can talk more afterwards, Dennis. There's so much I want to know about Colin's childhood." Her face creased. "I want you to tell me *everything.*"

And with that nightmarish threat, she headed back inside, her rain-drenched black dress clinging to her body. The brute, however, remained by Dennis's side. Not even the knowledge that the oversized thug's name was Nigel made him feel better.

"Well," said Dennis. "We should probably go and listen to the speeches." The man didn't move. "For Jenny's sake."

Nigel shoved him. Not hard enough to knock him over, but enough to put him off-balance. "Keep yer dirty fuckin' paws aff Jenny. She's mine now, ken? No' yours, and no' Roddy's."

"Woah, fella. Think you've got the wrong end of the stick here." Dennis held up his left hand to display the wedding band. "I'm married, see?"

The man either wasn't listening, or he didn't understand. "She's mine. No' yours." He leaned closer, breathing toxic alcohol fumes directly into Dennis's face. "With Colin gone, she's rightfully mine."

"Okay, I'm sorry." His heart pounded. Was the man going to hit him?

Instead, Nigel stepped back. He gently slapped his palm against Dennis's cheek, then reached into his coat.

A gun, he's got a gun.

"I'm warning you," the man said, as he pulled a long knife from inside his coat. The blade was curved, with an ornate handle like an ancient ceremonial dagger. "Touch her one more time, and I'll fuckin' skin you alive."

4

DENNIS WAITED UNTIL THE SPEECHES HAD BEGUN BEFORE EVEN considering re-entering the pub. The brute's threat had shaken him. Skin him alive? Christ, he'd only stopped to use the bloody toilet! Why couldn't he have done as Mel suggested and peed in the woods? These people were all demented. Every last one of them.

In despair, he gazed longingly at the garden wall. His car sat no more than thirty feet away, but there was no way he could scale that wall without being torn to shreds by wire and glass. And the worst part? He needed to pee again.

He peered through the door, where the townspeople stood in rapt attention as Jenny spoke into a microphone that turned her pleasant speaking voice into a booming cacophony.

"I'll never forget that rainy Tuesday afternoon," she was saying, "when Colin walked in here with his balloon animals and changed my life." A pause, a sniff. "Changed *all* our lives."

"Here, here!" cried the crowd.

As curious as Dennis was about Colin's balloon animal

skills, he took his chance and slipped inside, taking the most circuitous route possible as he crept along the perimeter, keeping low and out of sight.

"I only got to know Colin for a short time before he was so abruptly taken from me," Jenny continued. "But in that period, I loved him enough for ten lifetimes."

Dennis scurried past the snooker table with his head down, sticking to the wall. From where he stood, he could see the little bell above the exit.

Almost there, he thought, and allowed himself a tense smile.

"But there is someone," said Jenny, "who knew Colin better than any of us. Better than his loving wife, even."

The words echoed throughout the pub.

"Dennis, are you there?"

He came to an abrupt halt. His stomach dropped, and he thought his heart might stop. Silence all around. He crouched lower. Maybe, if he remained perfectly still, she wouldn't—

"There he is!" Jenny shouted into the microphone, her distorted voice thundering through the speakers and causing a shriek of ear-piercing feedback. "At the back of the room!"

Everyone turned to him. *Everyone.* Unsure of what to do, Dennis waved at her.

"Come on up," she said. "Tell us about Colin, and share some of the good times you spent with him in Italy."

No.

No, no, no, no, no.

"Oh, maybe later," he called back. "This isn't a good—"

Insistent hands gripped his arms, pushing him, *urging* him towards the stage as sympathetic faces gazed benevolently upon him. Pockets of applause broke out, and then two men were lifting him by the armpits onto the tiny stage where Jenny waited.

"No, come on," said Dennis, fighting his natural urge to run screaming. He tried to smile, and ended up grimacing. "Please, I'm shy."

The men shoved him towards Jenny, and she embraced him like an old friend. Or perhaps a lover? She kissed him on the mouth, his lips resolutely sealed as her wet tongue sought entry. In the confusion, he felt her slip something cold and metallic into his hand, and when she stepped to the side, he looked down at the dented microphone, then out at the crowd of faces.

"Oh balls," he muttered.

"You got this," he heard Jenny say, her fingertips — deliberately? — brushing his bum.

With his anxiety spiralling, he gazed out in confusion and horror. Could he do it? Could he drop the mic and run? No, there were too many people in the way. Far too many. He thought about Mel, and how she would never believe this ever-increasing catalogue of absurdity.

No one said anything. They were waiting for him to begin.

Dennis tapped the mic, causing three violent explosions of sound to erupt from the speakers. The crowd winced in unison, and he lifted the microphone to his dry lips.

"Hello," he said.

Was that enough? Could he go now?

Don't be ridiculous.

"My name is Dennis. You don't know me, but... I was friends with Colin."

"Best friends!" shouted Jenny.

"That's right. Best friends. We go way back, Colin and I. Boy, could I tell you some stories about him."

Don't say that! You'll set expectations too high!

"But, uh, most are unrepeatable."

"Go on, tell them!" someone called out.

"We're all adults here!" yelled another.

Sweat dripped down Dennis's neck. "Yeah, okay. Maybe I will." He faked a chuckle. "There's just so many to choose from."

Every eyeball in the pub was trained on him. Even the barman's, who polished a glass and frowned angrily.

Why is this happening?

"So, I remember this one time, we were on our way to school. We had to, uh, walk through this big field, and—"

"I thought you went to school in the middle of Rome?" Jenny interjected.

Dennis was a pacifist, but at that moment, he wanted nothing more than to punch her in the teeth.

"Yeah, we did," he said. "Good old Rome. When in Rome, do as the Romans do, that's what they say." He sighed. "Rome, huh? The city of love. Or is that Paris? I can never remember. They're both quite romantic, I think."

You're babbling.

"Anyway, there we were, walking through one of the most famous Romanian fields... no, wait, that's not right... umm, we walked through a field in Rome. Rome has fields, okay?"

He tasted vomit in the back of his throat.

"So, what was I saying... oh yeah, the field. Umm..."

He wanted to cry.

Where the hell was he going with this 'field' story? What sort of amusing hi-jinx ever happened in a field?

"Okay, scrap that. It wasn't a field. It was a—"

"Get to the point!"

Shit, they were heckling him now.

"I'm trying to... I'm just... I'm all broken up. Colin and me... the times we spent together were some of the happiest of my life. Rome has, uh, great nightlife, you know. We used to go to clubs to pick up girls, and this one time—"

Jenny spoke up again. "Didn't Colin leave Italy when he was fourteen?"

"He did. But, uh, the age of consent is lower in Italy."

There were audible gasps.

"I mean the *drinking* age. We weren't having sex. Ummm, I don't mean with each other. I mean with women. We weren't... look, we weren't having *any* sex, okay?"

Good god.

He no longer wanted to run, or to throw up. Now he wanted to die. A natural born introvert, this was his worst nightmare brought screaming to life.

It had to end. He needed to come clean and tell these people the truth before he completely lost control of the lie.

Maybe they'd see the funny side?

"I'm sorry," he said. His head started to swoon. "I can't do this, I just can't." Running a hand through his hair, he gripped the mic and carefully enunciated the words, *"I don't know Colin."*

Total silence. Someone coughed.

"Do you understand?" asked Dennis. "I *do not know* Colin."

"I don't suppose any of us did," said Jenny. "Not really."

"Aye, that's true," someone said. *"Well spoken, lad."*

Murmurs of approval. Scattered applause. What was happening? Dennis looked around. The crowd visibly edged closer, as if expecting some profound nugget of wisdom.

"I guess," he said, his mind racing, "you can *never* really know someone. You might, uh, *think* you do, but, in life, there's never time."

A lady dabbed at her eyes with a tissue.

It was the perfect moment to deliver the killing blow. He held the mic close and said, with as much false emotion as he could muster, "There's simply *never... enough... time.*"

A few of the grim faces nodded.

What, that wasn't sufficient? They needed more?

"But you know what Colin would have said at a time like this, don't you?"

He hoped so, because he didn't have a clue.

The crowd laughed. Not a lot, but enough to embolden him. He isolated one smiling, teary-eyed young woman, and pointed at her. "She knows what I'm talking about, am I right?"

A few snickers, a couple of chuckles.

"Come on," he said, desperate for her to give him a way out of this mess. "Tell us what Colin would have said."

The young woman shrugged good-naturedly. "He'd say, *help, she's hurting me!*"

That got the crowd going. Dennis watched laughter ripple through them. Private jokes were always impenetrable to an outsider, but he rolled with it.

"Yeah, classic Colin," he laughed. "Always asking for help." He turned serious. "But he was the first to offer it, wasn't he?"

"So true," said Jenny, and she blew her nose. "He was the first man to tell me I was beautiful after Gary died."

"And you all know what Colin would have said about *that!*" said Dennis, throwing it back to the crowd.

"He'd say, *please, I want to go home!*" laughed someone in a mocking tone.

"*I have a wife and child,*" shouted another. "*You can't do this to me!*"

They were in stitches. Absolute hysterics.

It's going well. End it, now!

"And so, I think we can all agree the world is a little sadder without our Colin in it. So please, join me in a toast."

He looked for a drink, and Jenny put her arm around him. "We can share mine," she said over the laughter, and together, they raised the glass.

"To Colin," said Dennis, and the response was deafening.

"To Colin!"

They drank, and Dennis realised he still had the mic in his hands. How to sign off? He knew. Play into their weird in-jokes, as if he understood.

"And so," he said, "in the words of my dear, departed friend Colin... *please, I want to go home!*"

That almost brought the house down. The crowd burst into hearty applause, and Dennis couldn't resist one more.

"I have a wife and child!" he said in an inexplicable Irish accent, and the place went nuts. Jenny hugged him tighter, and when he turned to her, she kissed him again. Her mouth closed over his, her tongue probing deeper this time. He had to stop her — he was married, for Christ's sake — but what could he do? Push her away? In front of everyone? No way! He had won them over, and surely, as long as he didn't upset anyone else, he could leave now?

And so he returned the kiss. She tasted of lipstick and tears, and she was one hell of a kisser.

"Okay, okay," he laughed, stepping back and keeping her at bay. "That'll do."

"I'm sorry." She stroked his face. "I can't seem to help myself around you."

Dennis wondered what the onlookers thought of the young widow sucking his face off, but when he gazed out, most had gone back to drinking and shouting. A man in a tweed hat approached the stage with an acoustic guitar.

"Off you trot, young lovers," he trilled. "The dance floor belongs to me, now."

They hopped down, and when Jenny pulled him close and told him she was going to buy him a drink, Dennis realised he was buzzing from adrenaline. His speech had gone down like gangbusters, and to have a receptive audience laughing along with him, and not *at* him, was an unfamiliar, but very welcome thrill. Jenny whispered something in his ear, but the music had started, and he couldn't quite hear.

"What did you say?" he shouted, leaning closer. "It's too loud!"

"I said," she laughed, then put her lips to his ears and whispered, "*I want to take you home and fuck your stupid brains out.*"

5

ALTHOUGH HE WASN'T PROUD OF IT, FOR A MOMENT DENNIS — still basking in the glory of a well-delivered speech — briefly considered Jenny's offer.

I want to fuck your stupid brains out.

The more he looked at her nymph-like face, the more he found she possessed an uncommon, almost ethereal beauty. Plus, she was a great kisser, and she smelled *divine*. How often did a proposal like this come along? He allowed his hands to move to Jenny's hips, his fingers finding her underwear through the flimsy fabric of her dress. His groin stirred, and when she tilted her head up to him and kissed him again, his groping hands slid further down, coming to rest on her chubby, round—

No!

Jesus Christ, what was he thinking? Was he really planning on cheating on his wife, who had stood by him during his darkest hours, and who loved him, and who he loved dearly?

Never. Absolutely not. The fact he had even entertained the idea appalled him. He was ashamed of himself.

And yet...

His hands lingered on her bottom, for Dennis was no fool. What was this, if not the perfect opportunity to escape? If he played along with Jenny, and *pretended* he wanted to sleep with her, then maybe, just maybe, he would be allowed to leave the pub. And the moment he was free from these four walls, he would hightail it to his car without ever looking back.

The chance had presented itself, and he was gonna grab it with both hands.

Literally.

"I'd like that," he said between kisses. "I'd like that a lot." He let his hands linger noncommittally on the voluptuous curves of her arse.

"Oh my god," she breathed, and kissed his neck. "Let's do it here. Right now, in front of everyone."

He hadn't expected *that*.

"Umm, I'd rather go somewhere private, if you don't mind. Just you and me would be great."

"Yes, yes, tell me more." Her hand burrowed into the waistband of his corduroys, and he insistently batted it away. "Once you've got me alone... what do you plan on *doing* to me?"

"Ummm... I'm going to kiss you all over."

She moaned orgasmically. "Where, though? Where will you kiss me? Tell me, Dennis."

"Jeez, I don't know. Your boobs." No, that didn't sound sexy. Pillow talk had never been his forte.

"And what about between my legs? Would you grant me that honour? Will you plant your seed deep inside my belly and allow it come to fruition?"

Dennis squirmed in discomfort. "Uh, sure. If that's what you're into."

"It's all I've *ever* wanted," she said, and passionately caressed his chest through his cardigan.

God, how much further would he have to debase himself?

"We should go," he said, trying not to sound like he was pleading. "Do you live nearby?"

"The far end of the village. Oh, but I can't leave now! It's Gary's wake."

"Don't you mean Colin?"

"Oh, yeah." She smiled at him from beneath the ram's skull. He wondered if she planned to keep it on during the sex they were absolutely *not* going to have. "I forgot. But we still have to stay until midnight." She traced her finger over his lips. "Can you wait for me that long, lover? Can you wait another few hours before making passionate love to me?"

"It'll be tough, but I guess I'm just gonna have to," said Dennis. His mind whirred. "Though... if we have to wait, I *do* need to fetch something from my car."

All traces of seduction left her voice. "What?"

"My phone, that's all."

"You don't need to phone me. I'm right here."

The change in her demeanour frightened him.

"I know that, baby." He kissed her, and gave her bum a cheeky slap, hating himself for doing so. "But I'm expecting a very important call."

That's it. Keep telling those lies, you mastermind!

"A call from who?"

"From a client. It's about a, uh, business deal. There's a lot of money at stake."

"And they're calling at this hour?"

"That's right. They're in Mumbai."

Wait, was Mumbai ahead of or behind UK time? He didn't know, and prayed she wouldn't either. Considering one of the guests had never heard of Edinburgh, he thought he was on pretty safe ground.

Jenny pouted as she pondered the information. "Okay. I believe you." She smiled warmly. "Go get your phone, and I'll order us some drinks. But not too many," she said, with a wink that reminded Dennis of the woman's mother. "You're gonna need *all* your stamina for the great impregnation."

"Well, that sounds... sexy." He took an uneasy step back, and gestured vaguely towards the door. "Cool. So, I'm gonna go now."

"You do that."

"Just gonna grab my phone from the car and come right back. I'll only be a minute, okay?"

You're babbling again.

He couldn't stop.

"And then, when I come back, I'm going to kiss you some more. All over your body. Yeah, uhh, I'm gonna have so much sex with you."

Okay, enough. She gets it.

"I look forward to it," said Jenny.

It was getting awkward. Even Jenny looked like she wanted him to leave.

"Well," he said, his cheeks burning. "In that case, see you in a minute!" He touched her nose, said, "Le boop," and walked away as she giggled. When he looked over his shoulder, she was on her way to the bar, swaying from inebriation.

Oh god, it's happening.

He kept going.

You're leaving.

As casually as possible, Dennis made his way to the door, gratefully accepting the compliments of those he passed on his exceptional speech.

"Please, I want to go home!" one of them guffawed, clapping Dennis on his back. "Classic Colin."

"Totally," Dennis laughed. He still didn't understand the joke.

The door was six feet away. No thugs blocked his path, no lunatic mothers accosted him, and no grieving widows offered their wombs for his seed.

Two more steps.

He reached the door. Gripped the handle.

Tremors rumbled through his limbs.

Locked. It's gonna be locked.

He tugged the handle. Overhead, the bell tinkled. Dennis paused and looked back. No one was watching. No one cared he was going. In disbelief, he stepped outside and closed the door, abruptly quietening the folk music and the raised voices. It felt too good to be true, and he waited in the rain for the door to fly open and several men to drag him inside, kicking and screaming. When that didn't happen, he turned left and strode to his car, watching the shadows dance and twirl in the windows.

What are you doing? Get out of here!

But something felt off. It was too easy.

Easy? You've been stuck in the ninth circle of hell for the last hour. You've been threatened, humiliated, and physically and sexually assaulted.

He couldn't argue with that. A lifetime of trauma crammed into one evening; those lunatics had unwittingly cost him a small fortune in future therapist bills.

Never mind.

He was free of them now.

Forever.

Fishing the keys from his pocket, he unlocked the car with the press of a button. It beeped cheerily at him, and he opened the door and took a seat, jamming the keys in the ignition. Rain battered the windscreen, and he removed his wet cardigan and tossed it onto the passenger seat.

He checked his phone. Seventeen missed calls from Mel. He tapped the screen to respond, and she answered immediately.

"Dennis? Where were you? I was so worried!"

The sound of her voice was heavenly. He reached for the keys to start the car. "Babe, you are not gonna *believe* what—"

Then the door was wrenched open, and someone roughly hauled him from the vehicle and threw him to the wet ground. He landed painfully on his knees, and squinted through the rain at the twisted, grimacing face of Nigel, the man who had promised to skin him alive.

He struck Dennis in the jaw with one meaty fist. A dazzling explosion of stars exploded across his vision, and Dennis, who was not used to being punched, toppled onto his side like a felled tree.

"I fucking warned you," Nigel growled. "She's mine."

Before he could respond, the brute booted him in the ribs.

"I saw you, you wee cunt. Fucking snoggin' ma Jenny's face off! I told you she's mine!"

He kicked him again. This time, Dennis thought he heard something break.

"Couldn't keep your grubby wee hands off her, could ye? Did it feel good, aye? Did her arse feel good?"

Mel's voice called out to him from inside the vehicle. *"Denny? You there? What's happening?"*

Help, he wanted to shout, but he couldn't speak, could hardly even breathe, as Nigel aimed kick after brutal kick at his unprotected face and torso.

The man reached into his coat, sliding the long dagger free. He held it in one oversized fist.

And as Dennis's eyes flickered shut, and the reflection of the lights in the puddles faded to darkness, he heard the sharp *thwick, thwick* of metal penetrating flesh, before the rush of hot blood splattered messily across his face.

6

————————

"DENNIS? ARE YOU OKAY?"

Sitting in the small flat she shared with her husband, Mel Norris gripped the phone hard enough to turn her knuckles white. The sound cut in and out, and all she heard between the pops and glitches was distant shouting, drowned out by the relentless patter of heavy rain on the car roof.

"Are you still there?"

Nothing. Why would he call her and then not speak? What if he'd been in an accident?

Not again, please, not again.

"Dennis, if you can hear me, say something!"

Rain. All she heard was rain.

"Dennis!" she cried. *"Answer me!"*

Over an hour had passed since he'd stopped to use the bathroom.

In a pub.

Booze was always involved somehow, wasn't it? He'd probably had a drink, then skidded off the road and—

No.

As far as she knew, her husband hadn't touched a drop in two years. What would cause him to break that streak now? Perhaps something his mother had said? That didn't sound right. Dennis's mum was a kind old soul who doted on the two men in her life; her son, Dennis, and her maniac pug, Big Baby. Mel doubted the woman had ever spoken a cruel word to anyone.

She hung up, and redialled in case it had been a bad line due to the patchy service in the north. The phone rang, and rang, and rang... and went to voicemail.

"Hey," she said, trying to sound calm. "It's me again. Give me a call when you can. I'm... look, just call, please." She paused. "I love you."

She tried to recall the name of the pub. The *something* inn. She wracked her brain, but the answer eluded her. It would come. And when it did, she would call and ask if they had seen her husband. Or if he was still there.

For now, she would do her best to relax.

There was nothing to be concerned about.

Nothing at all.

When he found the time, Dennis would call. He always did. He was a devoted, loving husband. Sure, he had made mistakes in the past, but who hadn't? Together, they had worked on rectifying them. That's what couples did. They helped each other. They loved each other.

And most important of all, they trusted each other.

She placed the phone on the armrest of the couch and turned the ringer volume up high.

"He'll call," she said, and went back to half-watching *Doctor Who*. She burst into tears. "He *always* calls."

7

At last, the nightmare was over.

When Dennis awoke, he was in his comfortable bed, his naked body snuggled against his wife's. She lay across his right arm, and his palm lightly cupped her breast. The closeness had given him a mighty erection, which nestled snugly between her buttocks, and though his head hurt, and his ribs ached like hell, he was back where he belonged.

No more speeches, no more kicks from Nigel... and no more paying respects to Jenny.

God, *Jenny*. He swore he could still taste her. What would he tell Mel? Or had he already done so? He couldn't recall getting home. The last thing he remembered was Nigel dragging him out of the car and kicking the ever-living shit out of him.

The morning light stung his eyes through the tightly sealed lids. Hugging Mel closer, he touched his left hand to his tender cheek. It hurt like hell. He struggled to breathe properly, and found cotton wool stuffed into his nostrils. God, he must be a total state. He removed one cotton ball and opened his eyes to inspect the damage, and that was when, instead of his wife's blonde hair, he saw the shock of brown locks before his eyes.

No...

He remained motionless, his eyes darting around the room. Daylight streamed in through gauzy curtains, illuminating unfamiliar pale pink walls decorated with photographs, and an antique wardrobe next to an equally weathered dressing table and chair, upon which hung a creased... black... dress.

"Oh fuck," he breathed.

Dennis wasn't given to swearing, but these extraordinary circumstances justified it. That was not Mel in his arms; his wife, who loved him, and who had helped him back from the brink after he had lost his job and almost his life to alcohol addiction.

No, this body — this naked, sweaty body — belonged to Hard Luck Jenny.

Dennis flinched, and the woman stirred. He clamped his eyes shut, as if that would do any good, and waited for her to settle. In a matter of seconds, she was breathing softly again. Suddenly realising where his right hand rested, he released the woman's bare breast and flattened his arm against the mattress.

What had he done? Had he cheated on Mel? He would never! Had Jenny drugged him? Or — and how he hoped and prayed this was the case — had she brought him home to take care of him after his assault? Should he be grateful for her kindness and hospitality?

That's an interesting definition of hospitality.

Fair point. He had to get out of here. The sun was up, and Mel would be freaking the hell out. God, he was such a fuck-up.

She'll understand once she sees your bruises. And you don't need to mention the fact you woke up with your cock sandwiched between a stranger's arse cheeks.

Okay, okay, what now? Pain flared through his neck when he turned his head to glance at the door. All he had to do was free his arm and sneak out without waking Jenny. He leaned back, testing her weight. The limb was stuck, but the pillow provided some wiggle room. Shuffling as far from her slumbering form as he could manage, Dennis pulled. Their dry skin rubbed together, and she groaned pleasantly. Was she hungover enough that he could he lift her without waking her? Last night, she had seemed pretty out of it. If his nose still worked, he imagined she'd smell of sweat and cigarette smoke and sweet, sweet alcohol. God, what he'd give for a drink right now.

Stop it!

Placing his left hand between her shoulder blades, he gently, oh so gently, pushed her forwards as he slid his arm back. If he could get as far as his elbow, the rest would follow.

Hopefully.

Outside, birds chirruped their morning song, and he heard a lawnmower or a hedge trimmer or some other garden tool. He moved Jenny further forwards, worried he'd shove her right off the bed like in that episode of *Friends* Mel loved. She used to tease him about it, because he was the one who enjoyed snuggling, not her.

Stop reminiscing and hurry up!

Jeez, he was sweating. A car sped by outside, and Jenny sighed, raising her head. Dennis took the opportunity and yanked his arm free.

"Mmmm," she said, her head flopping onto the pillow, and then she was sleeping again, and Dennis was up and out of bed, his heart thudding out of control.

Mission accomplished.

He found his glasses on the bedside table, but his clothes were elsewhere. He searched the floor. No trousers, no shirt, no socks or boxers or even shoes. They had to be *somewhere*. On his tiptoes, he made his way around the bed. Jenny's black thong and a pair of tights lay on the carpet, but none of his belongings. Dammit, where were his clothes? He couldn't walk down the street to the car with his bare arse on show.

Could he?

The door was open a crack, and he shambled towards it, his body in torment. The morning light revealed the full damage Nigel had inflicted on him. Large purple bruises smothered his torso and legs, and several of the kicks had broken his skin.

The floor creaked beneath him, and he winced.

"Huhwho'sthaaah?" said Jenny, her voice hard and cracked.

Dennis didn't move. He waited, stark naked, with one leg bent uncomfortably and starting to cramp, until he was sure she was asleep.

"Okay," he breathed, and walked with aching slowness towards the door. He pulled it open, waiting for the hinges to squeak, but — oh merciful maker! — they never did. Closing the door behind him, he found himself in a hallway. The plush green carpet was soft beneath his feet, and at the far end he spotted a glass-panelled front door. He considered making a break for it, and decided to find something to wear first. Jenny was out for the count, and he did not wish to get arrested for indecent exposure the second he left the house.

He shuffled noiselessly to the nearest door. His head

swooned, and he leaned against the wall, blood dripping from his nose and down his face and chest.

You are not okay to drive.

Nope. But he sure as hell wasn't planning on hanging around here any longer, where he was either going to be murdered by Nigel or end up married to Jenny. In a strange way, he sympathised with the woman. He supposed she could chalk this up to another case of her bad luck.

Ignoring the stabbing pain in the middle of his face, he pushed open the door and entered a bathroom so clean it could be a showroom. The metalwork of the taps and towel rail gleamed in light that streamed through the large window, while the towels themselves hung perfectly straight, as if Jenny had used a set-square to get the angles just right. Only a couple of dark red stains on the bathmat indicated someone actually lived here.

Out of curiosity, he took a look at himself in the mirror.

He wished he hadn't.

The battered face that greeted him turned his stomach. One eye was severely swollen. Dried blood caked his mouth and chin, and ugly bruises marred one side of his face. Admittedly, he'd looked worse after the car crash, but he sure wouldn't be winning any beauty pageants in the near future.

The urge to wash his face and clean the blood off was strong, but not as powerful as his desire to get home, so he left the bathroom and carried on down the hallway in search of his missing clothes. Behind the next door was a store cupboard with various cardboard boxes piled from floor to ceiling. Names were scrawled on each box in black marker. GODFREY, ANDREAS, ANNE, SZYMON, GARY... and resting atop them all was one that read COLIN.

The words of Jenny's mother rang in his ears.

Colin's the third one she's lost this year.

With a shudder, he headed to the adjacent door and gently turned the handle, stepping into an immaculate kitchen. Like the bathroom, it had been scrubbed and polished to within an inch of its life. Brass handles sparkled on the wood-panelled cupboards, the pots and dishes stacked on the drying rack above—

The washing machine!

Of course! It was open, the glass door wet as if recently emptied.

"Yes," he said, and walked stiffly towards it on ponderous limbs, wondering if—

"Oh look, Myrtle, he's up!"

Dennis turned sharply. The movement made him sway, and he reached out and caught the countertop before he could fall, his groggy eyes struggling to focus on the two women seated at the table.

Two women?

Shit.

His heart sank as he recognised Jenny's mother, Roberta. She sat next to a younger woman of a similar age to Jenny. Her sister? Oh, what did it matter! He covered his genitals with one hand, using the other for balance. "I'm sorry," he said, trying to sound as nonchalant as possible, "but I don't suppose either of you have seen my clothes?"

"Such an early riser," Roberta said, and took a sip of her coffee as if a naked man interrupting her breakfast routine was an everyday occurrence.

"My clothes. Have you seen them?"

The younger woman — Myrtle, Roberta had called her — giggled behind her hand at his state of undress. Dennis wanted to crawl into a hole and die. He rested against the counter and used both hands to cover his nakedness.

"Och, you needn't hide yourself," said Roberta. "I've seen a man's willy before!"

"I haven't," said the younger woman. She turned to Roberta. "Mum, are they always so small?"

"Sometimes they are, but maybe Jenny's new friend is a wee bit shivery."

"It's not small," he said feebly, then caught himself. This was not the hill he was willing to die on. "Please, I need something to wear."

Roberta ignored him. "You can make it longer by giving it a rub," she explained. "That gets the blood flowing in all the right places."

"Can I have a go?"

Roberta laughed. "Well, we should check with Jenny first."

"Share and share alike, that's what you always—"

"My clothes, *please!*" snapped Dennis. The two women halted their discussion and looked at him. He lowered his voice. "Where are they?"

"Why, I had to wash your filthy old clothes," said Roberta. "You made a real mess of yourself last night. Blood and sick everywhere! Poor Myrtle here had to hand-scrub your underpants."

"They smelled funny," the younger woman said.

Jesus Christ, they're all insane.

"Okay," said Dennis, trying to act like the only reasonable and calm adult in the room. "So you washed them." He took a breath. "And where are they now?"

"Why, in the garden, of course. Where else would I hang them on a lovely sunny day?"

"Great." He smiled, and started shuffling towards the door. "I'll go get them, and be on my way. Thank you for—"

"They won't be dry yet," said Roberta. "I only put them out an hour ago."

"That's fine." He bumped into the doorframe. "I don't mind."

"Are you sure I can't rub your willy?" Myrtle called. "Just for a minute, to see if I can make it—"

But Dennis had already ducked out of the room. He glanced down the hall. There was no back exit, so he jogged to the front door and tried the handle.

Locked.

"Oh, come *on*." He rattled the handle. Shook it, yanked on it. But the door remained shut. He turned to find the two women standing in the hallway watching him. "How do I get out of here?"

"With the keys, silly," said Roberta.

"I know that," he snapped. "Where the fuck are they?"

"Mind your language in front of Myrtle," Roberta reprimanded him.

"Well, could you ask her to stop staring at me?"

"Says the man wandering around in the scud," Roberta said dismissively, and she and her daughter laughed. "And anyway, you can't go outside with your wee willy out. What would the neighbours think? I'll bring your clothes in once they're dry."

If Dennis's hands hadn't been cupped over his genitals, they would have tightened into fists. These women were toying with him. "Bring them in *now*," he snarled. They laughed at him, and there was nothing — absolutely *nothing* — he could do about it. He was naked, his body broken and bleeding, and he didn't know where he was, and the only people able to help him were utterly, psychotically deranged.

"Come on through to the kitchen," Roberta said, "and

I'll make you beans on toast. You look like you need a hearty meal."

"And then can I play with his willy?" asked Myrtle.

"You'll have to ask your sister when she wakes up."

"No one," said Dennis, "is playing with... is playing with *anything*. Any part of me. It's *all* off-limits."

"Bet he never said that to Jenny last night," said Myrtle, as the women wandered back into the kitchen, chuckling to themselves and leaving Dennis standing by the front door.

Did they expect him to follow? He had to be out of here before Jenny woke up! He swallowed, and tasted blood.

The bathroom. He would head there and freshen up, then grab a towel to cover himself while he plotted his next move. Down the hall he staggered, barging into the bathroom and almost collapsing. It felt like a grim flashback to his days of alcoholism. He took a long drink from the tap and spat out a mouthful of murky, blood-flecked water into the pristine sink. His throat hurt. Even his gums throbbed. Upon closer inspection in the mirror, he noticed two teeth were missing. He prodded the gaps with his tongue and uttered a low moan.

Shit. In the unforgiving glare of the early morning sun, he—

Wait.

Gingerly, he turned towards the frosted glass window through which the light poured. It was tall, and split into upper and lower sections. Would they open? And could he possibly fit through?

He closed the bathroom door. There was no lock, which was not unexpected for this family of maniacs, so he would have to be quick. Stepping onto the toilet seat, he unclasped a latch between the panes. The lower portion was fixed shut, but with enough pressure, the top half slid partway down. Through the gap, Dennis looked out at the verdant landscape. Beneath a clear blue sky, pine trees glistened with yesterday's raindrops, and a winding country road led through rolling hills of fields. He started to cry, and tugged the window down further. It was tricky to move — he doubted it had ever been opened this wide — and the space between the windows and the frame amounted to no more than ten inches.

A knock at the door.

"Are you alright in there, Little Darling Dennis? Do you need any help?"

"Not from you, bitch," he muttered, and reached through the gap. A light breeze tickled his arms, and it felt wonderful. His head followed, then his shoulders. He saw the garden, and the washing line upon which his clothes hung from colourful pegs. The sight galvanised him, and he pushed his feet against the glass to gain more height. His belly scraped painfully across the window frame, and he sucked his gut in.

Almost there!

He was halfway through. Now what? How was he going to get down without breaking his neck?

Another knock.

"Right, I'm coming in."

To hell with that. Wriggling his hips, he forced his way through until he could no longer support his own weight. His upper torso swung like a pendulum, slamming his face against the glass with enough force to crack it. His palms touched the window sill, and then he was tumbling forwards, his legs arcing in a clumsy flip.

Convinced he was going to shatter his skull, Dennis closed his eyes and let gravity take over. His heels cracked off a concrete slab, and his lower back scratched viciously against the sill... but he was out.

Roberta's blurry silhouette hammered its fists against the frosted glass. *"Just where do you think you're going, young man?"*

"Up yours, bitch!" he shouted, and raised his middle finger, pressing it against the window, right in front of her face. "I'll see you in—"

"My wife raises an important point, son."

Shocked, Dennis looked over his shoulder at the bearded man in the crisp shirt, then down to the shotgun he cradled menacingly in both hands. The barrel pointed directly at him.

"Precisely where *do* ye think yer going?"

8

THE COLD STEEL OF THE SHOTGUN PRODDED DENNIS'S LOWER back.

"Yer no plannin' on runnin' out on ma wee Jenny, are ye?" growled her father while his wife continued hammering on the window. "Dinnae worry, love," he shouted. "The slippery bastard's no' goin' anywhere."

"You're making a mistake," said Dennis. The barrel pressed harder into his spine. "I'm just trying to go home."

"You *are* home. Now put both hands on your head and face me like a man."

Tears fell as Dennis complied with the order. "What do you want from me?"

So close. He had been *so close*.

The old man stared at him. It was almost disappointing how normal he looked. With his pink shirt buttoned all the way up and a smart side-parting and neatly trimmed beard, he could be any typical out-of-shape dad mowing the grass on a Monday morning.

"What do you think I want?" His tense posture relaxed.

"I want you to make my Jenny the happiest bride in the land."

"Bride?" Dennis bristled. *"Bride?* I'm already married, you fucking lunatic!"

The man lowered the shotgun barrel from Dennis's midriff... but only as far as his crotch. "Listen, I've already spent a lot of money on this wedding. My wife was on the phone all morning, making the arrangements. We've booked The Rockarn Inn for tonight, and Myrtle's ironed you and Jenny's wedding dresses."

"What... what are you *talking* about? What the fuck are you talking about? I only stopped to use the bathroom, and you people have kept me here against my will. You've abused me, you've humiliated me, and now you're telling me—"

Crack!

Jenny's father moved surprisingly fast for his age. He spun the shotgun and smacked the wooden stock against Dennis's cheek.

Holding his face, Dennis stumbled against the wall. "You... you can't do this. You can't keep me here."

"No one's *keeping* you here, you wee smout. But you made a promise, and you're going to keep it. Maybe that's not how you do things in the big city, but—"

Footsteps crunched on the gravel path around the side of the building.

"Shush now," the man said. "Here comes Jenny, and I dinnae want you upsettin' her with your silly notions."

"This is crazy," Dennis muttered. "You're all crazy."

Jenny appeared around the corner in frayed denim cutoffs and a cropped tee. She placed her hands on her hips and chuckled sweetly.

"Daddy, *why* are you pointing a gun at my Dennis?"

"No reason, dear," he said, his voice losing its hard edge. "Havin' a wee man-to-man chat, that's all."

"Aww, so cute." She walked to Dennis and wrapped her arms around his bare chest, kissing his cheek. "I'm surprised you're up, lover. How do you feel?"

"Oh, I'll tell you how I feel." He wanted to shove her to the ground, but with the shotgun pointed at him, he was impotent. "I feel like shit, and I want to go home."

She chuckled. "Oh Dennis, you and your jokes. You know, you really should put some clothes on." She playfully flicked his shrivelled penis. "You want my sister to see you like that?"

"Too late!" laughed Myrtle.

"She already saw him in the kitchen!" added Roberta, who stood beside her daughter with her arm draped over her shoulder. Dennis hadn't even noticed their arrival.

Great, he thought. *The whole family's here.*

With his hands fixed on his head, he angled his body in a futile attempt to hide himself. "Look, I don't know what kind of sick game you're playing, but I think it's gone a little too far now, don't you?"

"Game?" Jenny looked confused. "What game?"

Dennis watched the father's face harden. "What I mean is, there's been a misunderstanding. Your father is under the impression that you and I are getting married."

"But we are! It's happening tonight. Aren't you excited? All your friends from the village are invited."

"Can I touch his willy?" asked Myrtle.

Dennis ignored them both. "We can't marry, Jenny, because I'm *already* married, and have been for thirteen years. My wife's name is Melanie, and if you let me call her, she can attest to everything I'm telling you."

"Silly!" said Jenny. "Your stupid sham marriage counts for nothing round here."

"Our ways are different to your own." Roberta spoke to him like he was an idiot. "Simpler. More... primal."

"When you spilled Nigel's blood on behalf of Jenny," her father said, "that amounted to a proposal."

"And I accepted," Jenny added, "by making love to you."

What were they talking about? What the giddy *fuck* were they *talking* about? His body shook as he started to panic.

"Okay, okay, okay," he said, his cheeks wet with tears. He turned to Jenny. "First of all, we did not make love last night. We did *not* have sex."

"Oh Dennis, how can you say that?"

"You scrawny wee runt." Her dad stepped closer. "You *did* make love to my daughter." He smiled at his wife. "We both watched it happen, and it was a magical evening."

"Truly sensual," Roberta said. "It fair put *us* in the mood, I'll tell you that."

Myrtle pulled a face. "Ewww, mum!"

Dennis almost smiled at the absurdity of it all. The idea that Jenny's parents had watched as their mad daughter ground her hips atop his unconscious body was unfathomable, an image torn from a night terror. And yet... he believed them.

A strange sensation flooded his veins.

All his life, Dennis had tried to live as respectfully of others as possible, putting everyone else's needs ahead of his own. When someone got angry, he was quick to back down. If an apology was required, he was always the first to make it. Nothing was too much trouble if it meant keeping the peace. But even he had a limit, and now that limit had been breached. Not once, not twice, but multiple times. Normally, fear and embarrassment were his default emotions, constantly jostling for supremacy. But in the face of this insanity, this torture, their weight lifted like the soul leaving a dead body, and in their place was a less familiar feeling... one that seemed to cloud his mind like an impenetrable fog.

It was anger.

It was fury.

It was rage.

He glared at them. "You're sick, monstrous *fucks.*"

"Language, please," Roberta chided. "I've already told you, I won't have swearing in my—"

"Oh no, heaven forbid there's some fucking swearing in a house where parents watch their daughter rape a man while he sleeps!"

"It's not rape if he's spilled the blood of her enemy!" the father roared.

"What enemy? That man attacked me! It was my blood that was spilled, not his! *Look at me!*" He gestured at his battered body. *"Look at the fucking state of me!"*

The family fell silent, until the father nodded conspiratorially and said, "Clever boy. I see what you're doing."

"What do you mean, dad?" asked Myrtle.

Dennis was glad she'd asked, because he had no idea what the old bastard was on about.

"You know when a hedgehog curls intae a wee ball to protect itself?" her father began. "Well, that's what your brother Dennis is doing. He thinks he'll be caught for what he did to Nigel, and thrown intae jail."

"I didn't do anything to him," said Dennis, letting the 'brother' comment slide for now. "I was attacked, not him."

"Aye, you never touched him." Jenny's father tapped his finger against the side of his nose. "Mum's the word, eh?" He shook his head and laughed. "It's awright, son. You dinnae need to worry about the law. We look after our own." He nodded towards a rickety wooden shed in the corner of the garden. "Take a wee peek in there. I think you'll like what you see."

Rooted to the spot, Dennis stared at the shed. It lurked in the shadow of a rowan tree, the once-green paint chipped and peeling.

"Go on," the old man urged. "But keep your hands where I can see them until you reach the shed, and nae funny business."

Dennis staggered from the wall, unsure if his legs would carry him all the way. But what choice did he have? He wandered past the washing line and stared at his clothes. Never before had the sight of damp boxer shorts fluttering in the breeze made him feel like weeping.

He approached the shed. Thick cobwebs obscured the window panes, and a faint, unpleasant odour seeped from within. He looked back, praying they would all be gone, but the family followed at a discrete distance.

Lowering his hands, he turned the metal knob. With a groan, the shed door swung open, and Dennis brought his hand to his mouth. At first it was simply from the smell; a pungent, malodorous reek strong enough to penetrate his blood-caked nostrils. But as his eyes adjusted to the darkness, and he lowered his gaze, he started to heave.

There was Nigel, the man he had supposedly beaten up. His blood had been spilled, all right. It had been spilled in abundance.

Beneath a shelf of oil cans and pruning tools, the brute lay across a pile of logs, the skin on his cheeks hanging in shreds from multiple slashes and stab wounds. His throat had been hacked — not slit, but *hacked* — open, and the blood had congealed in the wound and soaked into the man's funeral attire. It was the first corpse Dennis had ever seen, and as he dropped to his knees and vomited on the lawn, he had a strong suspicion it would not be the last.

A shadow fell across his face. He looked up to see Jenny's father looming over him.

"Aye, you needn't worry. We look after our own round here." The man smiled thinly. "And you're part of the family now, Dennis."

What did he mean? What the hell did he mean? Did the bastard somehow think *he* had killed Nigel? That he had stabbed someone, over and over, plunging a knife into a dying man's screaming face, carving it open and hacking at his flesh until it hung from the bone?

He gazed vacantly into the pool of his own puke.

"I didn't do that," he said, spitting out a glob of vile-tasting phlegm. "I wouldn't kill. I *couldn't.*"

"But you *did* do it. You fought for my wee girl's honour, because you love her." He sighed. "It's like the old song says... in fae a pound, in fae a penny, aw the laddies love Hard Luck Jenny."

Dennis shook his head. A string of drool dangled from his busted lip, and he let it hang there until the liquid cord snapped. He felt like a fool on his hands and knees, naked and staring at his own splattered vomit. The rage simmering within began to boil over.

"I don't love her," he said. "I don't even *like* her."

"C'mon, lad. Dinnae be like that. We saw the way you ploughed her holy garden."

Roberta chimed in. "It was beautiful. It was love."

"No," snarled Dennis. "You're lying. I don't give a *fuck* about your daughter. In fact, I hate her."

Jenny started to cry, and Dennis grinned maniacally. He had hurt her, and it felt wonderful.

"Careful, son," her father said. "Choose your next words very, very carefully."

"I don't care anymore. You're murderers, a family of murderers. I hate you all." He turned to Jenny and wiped the puke-stained smile from his face. "But most of all, I hate *you*. I hate your face and your lies and your home and *every single one* of your stupid, dead husbands. I hope you rot in hell, because that's what you des—"

The ground exploded. Plumes of dirt and fresh vomit cascaded over Dennis, his ears ringing from the shotgun blast as dozens of birds took flight from the surrounding trees, shaking the branches and causing loose leaves to flutter into the garden.

"You know," Jenny's father said, "I've never lived in the city, so I don't know how you lot do things. But here, if a man spills blood for a woman, and she accepts that blood and gives him her body in return, then that's marriage. That's *love.*"

Dennis was too busy screaming to listen to the old fool's ravings. He screamed until his throat was raw, and then screamed some more. And when he could no longer scream — when his ravaged voice had utterly deserted him, and all that emerged was a desiccated croak — he curled up on the grass, his body limp, until he found the willpower to scream again. Could no one hear him? Did nobody care? He thought about last night's wake, and about how the whole village had been present. They had to have known something was amiss.

They're all complicit.

As terrible as that sounded, it made sense.

All of them.

He had to escape. No longer could he tiptoe around in shame, worried about causing a scene or making a fool of himself. Hell, he was lying naked on the grass and covered in his own vomit. How much more pathetic could he get?

He stared up at his new family.

"Alright," said Roberta sternly. "That'll be enough excitement for one morning. We've got a wedding to prepare for! Myrtle, you help me with the cake. Gordon, get on the phone and organise the flowers."

"What about me, mum?" asked Jenny.

The woman cast a disgusted glance at Dennis. "Fetch the hose and give your fiancé a rinse. Make sure you get into all the nooks and crannies. He can't get married in that state."

As he lay on the grass, Dennis closed his eyes and wondered; if he was to never rise again, how long it would take for his body to decompose into the earth?

Too long was the answer, and yet somehow it was still preferable to going through with this fraudulent wedding ceremony. He blamed his bladder for ending up here. All he had wanted was to pee. He was doing it now, the warm liquid spraying onto his thigh.

See? It's not that hard to go in front of people.

No, he supposed not.

Something prodded his stomach. He opened his eyes to find Jenny's father jabbing him with the shotgun.

"On your feet, son, and let's start anew. You're tired, that's all. Nigel must have put up a hell of a fight."

"Leave me alone," Dennis mumbled.

"Come on. You'll feel better with a full belly." The man rested the shotgun barrel on the ground, leaning on it like a cane. "My wife always says, breakfast is the most important meal of the—"

And that was the moment Dennis grabbed the barrel

with both hands. He yanked it out from under Jenny's father, causing the old man to fall onto his side.

This is it, he thought madly, and aimed the deadly weapon towards his bride-to-be, his body throbbing with adrenaline.

His finger found the trigger, and he broke out in a wide smile.

Time to go home.

9

Jenny was the first family member to react. Luckily, her response amounted to little more than a startled yelp as her father crashed heavily to the ground.

Rising to his knees, Dennis aimed the gun at his unwanted fiancée, staring down the cold, steel barrel at her petrified face. His temples throbbed, and his finger itched.

Could he do it?

After everything they had done to him, could he pull the trigger? If they forced his hand... could he kill?

Jenny shuffled closer.

"Stay away from me," he growled. "All of you, stay the fuck back!"

"Dennis!" Roberta shouted. "Why are you doing this?"

"Why? *Why?* Are you really asking me fucking *why?*" He backed up, keeping a distance between himself and the brood of psychopaths.

Clutching his side, Jenny's father got to his feet.

"Careful, dad," said Myrtle. "He's got a gun!"

"I fucking know that!"

"Well, why did you let him take it?"

71

"Yes, take the gun back, Gordon," said Roberta. "I have to start baking the wedding cake."

Dennis smiled.

Let them argue. Let them bicker amongst themselves, and cast blame on each other.

Those bastards.

He moved closer to the shed. Jenny's father followed, but as Dennis's finger hovered over the trigger, the man raised his hands.

"Dinnae be daft, now," the old bastard said. "Let's talk this out like men."

Dennis shifted his aim between Jenny and her father, concern creeping into their previously smug faces. He doubted he could kill them. That was a step too far, even after everything they'd done to him. Dennis believed in justice, and these monsters deserved a fair trial in a court of law, and then to spend the rest of their miserable lives in prison. But while *he* knew killing was out of the question, *they* certainly didn't, and he had to admit that being the one in control after all this time felt—

Jenny reached for the weapon, and he snatched it out of her grasping fingers, stepping quickly across the grass to where his clothes hung on the washing line.

"I'm warning you, I'll shoot!"

"What are you doing, Dennis?" asked Jenny. "You're going to be my husband!"

"Like hell I am. Do you even know my surname?"

She faltered. "Well... of course I do."

"Then what is it?"

"It's... Mac-something, isn't it?" She scrutinised his face for clues. "No, not Mac. Umm, Sutherland? Dennis... Rumplejack?" She looked to her family. "Can someone help?"

"I know his surname," said Myrtle. "I saw it on his credit card."

Jenny turned on her sister. "Why were you going through my fiancé's things?"

"Girls, we can discuss that later," their father interjected. He advanced on Dennis, his hands still raised. "Listen to me, son. We both ken you're no' gonnae shoot, so why not put the gun down and we'll all go in and have a nice breakfast together. Our first as a family."

"Stay back. I'll kill you all if I have to."

He hoped his threats didn't sound empty. Because if it came down to it, he would happily blow the old bastard's leg off at the knee if he had to.

"Come on, Dennis," said Jenny, "Give dad his gun back. You're acting like a real brat, and you're going to spoil the wedding."

"There's not going to be a fucking wedding! I already had one, and it was the best day of my life. So instead of pretending to marry a fucking lunatic, I'm going to go home, call the police, and tell them there's a dead man in your garden shed, and that *you,* Jenny, are the one who killed him to blackmail me into marrying you."

Roberta was next up to try to placate him. "Dennis, please. Put the gun down. There's bread in the toaster waiting for you."

"Oh, wow, *toast?* Why didn't you say so before!"

The woman looked genuinely offended. "Well, there's no need to be sarcastic."

He took another step back. Why did they keep coming? Why wouldn't they stay away like he asked? He wanted to grab his clothes from the washing line, but he couldn't risk taking his eyes off the family for even a second.

"Oh my god," said Myrtle, pointing between his legs. "It's gotten even smaller!"

He turned the gun on her. The family spread apart like a military operation. Jenny was getting too close.

"Stay back!" Dennis spun, aiming at her father, who was attempting to flank him. "Seriously, I'm warning you. All of you. Don't even think about—"

It was Jenny that leapt at him.

But she was too far away, and Dennis dodged out of her reach. He cracked the wooden stock against her skull, and she dropped, but in the time it took him to spin the weapon back into position, Myrtle had already lunged. Her fingers wrapped around the barrel as she tried to wrench it from his hands. For such a slight creature, she was shockingly strong. He pulled back, catching her off-balance and bringing her closer. Their foreheads struck, and as she stumbled backwards, Myrtle gave one final hard yank on the shotgun.

What Myrtle *hadn't* considered was that Dennis's finger was still curled neatly around the trigger. At least, not until the sharp tug brought the two elements together, and the resultant blast from the shotgun cut her messily in two.

10

———

Myrtle uttered a guttural grunt as her midsection exploded in a shower of blood, entrails, and shattered bone. At such close range, the detonation obliterated her from her waist to her breasts.

Her legs hit the ground first, her guts slopping onto the grass like a wet, hot salad. Myrtle's upper half thudded down a second later, her rigid fingers still gripping the shotgun barrel, an almost comically shocked expression carved into her face.

No one moved, not even as blood pattered onto the corpse like so many delicate crimson raindrops.

Dennis stared at the dead woman in shock.

Good god, he had killed her. *Murdered* her. Cut her down in the prime of her life. And in doing so, he had not only flown in the face of all his well-honed principles and morals... he had upended his entire belief system.

So what are you waiting for? Fucking run!

And run he did.

Screw his stupid principles; the time for reflection could come later. He leapt over Myrtle's splattered, steaming remains, but her claw-like hands clung to the shotgun barrel, and he realised he was dragging her upper half behind him, leaving a gruesome red trail on the freshly mown lawn. She was slowing him down, so he released the weapon and ran for the gravel path that led along the side of the cottage.

Gravel? Are you sure that's—

"Ah, shit!" he yelled, as dozens of sharp stones jabbed into his bare feet. But he didn't stop. He would never stop, not until he was safe. Were they following? He looked back, and the sapling next to his head erupted in an explosion of splintered bark.

Yeah, they were following.

And they had the gun.

Ignoring the pain in his exposed, bloody soles, Dennis raced along the side of the cottage, his cock bouncing with each frenzied step. He rounded the corner and ran into the front garden, heading for a path of concrete paving slabs. Rather than waste time opening the gate, he put his hands on the wrought iron and vaulted over onto the pavement. Now... where the fuck was he?

He stared straight ahead at a field dotted with cows, then—

The shotgun fired again, blowing a hole in the hedge the size of a bowling ball.

Left. He needed to go left.

"Put some clothes on, you pervert!" a woman shouted from her garden as he raced by. *"And what's all that racket?"* The road curved, and Dennis followed, hoping, *praying* his car would still be there.

And if they've moved it?

Then he would keep running. He would run all the way back to Durness on bleeding, torn feet if he had to.

Ahead, at the far end of the village, he saw the unassuming harled walls of the inn. The shutters were closed, the lights were off, and a single vehicle was parked outside. A blue Toyota Yaris, the number plate spattered with mud.

His blue Toyota Yaris.

He could have wept. Instead, he ran for his life, his feet making sharp clacking sounds from all the pebbles lodged in his soles. Each heavy step forced them deeper into his flesh, but there was no stopping him now.

He was almost at the car.

"Come on!" he screamed at himself. *"Come on!"*

It felt like a dream. What if it was? Perhaps he was still lying in bed with Jenny. He imagined her balancing atop him and frantically rubbing his cock while her parents — his future in-laws, apparently — watched hand-in-hand, smiling beatifically.

No. This couldn't possibly be a dream.

He was in too much pain.

Ahead, he glimpsed bright red through a hedge. He increased his pace, but as he neared, the gate swung open and a postman carrying a bulky red shoulder bag stepped out. Dennis recognised the man immediately. It was hard to forget the face of Roddy, the thug who had squeezed his balls until he cried.

The postie looked at him in confusion, doubtlessly surprised to see a naked man running full throttle towards him at this early hour of the morning. "Hey," he said, and dropped his bag, spreading his arms wide. "Stop right—"

The two men collided. Dennis's knee slammed into Roddy's testicles with a brutal crunch, and the bigger man toppled. He hit the pavement, but managed to wrap his burly arms around Dennis's leg.

"Help!" he shouted. "We've got another runner!"

Dennis tried to shake free. He looked back. Jenny's father struggled around the bend, his face beet red, one hand holding the shotgun, the other clamped over his heart.

"She's lost three husbands this year!" the postie shouted. "Think about her family!"

Jenny's father drew closer. He stopped, raised the shotgun, and changed his mind. "Let go of him, Roddy! I cannae get a clear shot!"

But Roddy clung on like moss to a tree, and out of sheer desperation, Dennis pressed his thumbs against the man's eyeballs, pushing them like he was trying to shove a cork back into a wine bottle. The man screamed — it was funny to hear a big hard-man scream like that — as Dennis forced his digits through the thin lids and into the juicy orbs. They seemed to deflate under the pressure, spilling sticky white goo down the man's cheeks.

Roddy released him and rolled onto his back, clawing at the gaping red craters where his eyes had once been.

Dennis left him there, and ran.

"Come back, ya wee cunt!" shouted Jenny's father.

"Like fuck," he spat, heading straight for his car. Now there was no one between him and his trusty vehicle. All he needed were his keys and...

Dennis almost skidded to a stop.

His keys.

The fucking keys to the car! Where were they? In his trouser pocket? In his jacket? On the kitchen counter in Jenny's house? They sure as shit weren't on him now.

He reached the Toyota, and, purely out of instinct, grabbed the release. The door opened, and there, dangling from the ignition, were his keys. He remembered now; getting in the car, calling Mel, and putting the keys in ready to drive, right before Nigel dragged him out and pummelled him.

Holy shit. Unlike Jenny, his luck was in!

Throwing himself into the driver's seat, he gunned the engine and stomped the accelerator. Ahead of him, the blinded postman staggered onto the road, grasping at his face and shrieking bloody murder.

"I've got a special delivery for you," muttered Dennis, and he spun the wheel, swerving the car. The postie thumped dully against the bonnet, smacking against the windscreen and loudly bumping over the roof. His broken body crumpled to the road, rolling twice before coming to a stop.

Dennis grinned madly.

One down...

He took aim at Jenny's father. The man had the shotgun raised, but when he saw what Dennis had in mind, he stumbled over the nearest wall and landed in a neighbour's garden, his legs arcing through the air. Dennis spun the wheel to change course, the metalwork screeching along the stone wall and shooting up sparks.

No problem. The police would deal with him. And by that, he meant the Edinburgh police, not some madcap local constabulary who would likely hand him over to Jenny's demented clan.

Hell, they're all in on it.

The hybrid vehicle chugged on, gaining speed. He drove past Jenny's home, and saw her standing by the gate, watching helplessly as he made his escape. She held her arm out as if flagging a taxi.

He lowered the window as he passed, shouting, *"Fuck you!"* and whooping with glee.

He was out.

God-fucking-dammit, he was *out*.

In the rearview, the village grew smaller. The inn, the row of cottages, the field, each diminishing in size until he entered thick woodland and the buildings vanished altogether. Trees sped by in a manic blur, but he refused to take his foot off the gas.

Slow down. Remember the accident.

As if he could ever forget.

It had taken place on a road similar to this one. Fired up on vodka and rum, he had raced home from an evening drinking alone in the pub after a school conference, desperate to be back in time for his anniversary dinner with Mel. He was already an hour late when he got in the car, and didn't actually arrive home until four months later, when he was finally discharged from hospital.

On that day, he had gathered his hidden bottles from around the house, emptied them into the sink, and sworn to Mel he would never touch another drop.

"Life is too precious to waste," he had broken down and told her. *"Especially life with you."*

He had meant it, too, and with his own words blaring insistently in his ears, he slowed the car from seventy to sixty miles-per-hour. Every few seconds, he checked the mirrors.

Nobody was following.

For now.

As he took the sharp bends at speed, he thought about what he would say to the police. Was there any way to keep the story out of the papers? If his pupils heard of his misadventures, he would become a laughing stock. He'd have to change his name, his appearance, even his school.

What about Myrtle? You gonna tell the police you killed her?

Obviously. That wasn't his fault. He was completely innocent.

And the postman? You can't call that self-defence. That was cold-blooded murder, plain and simple.

The more he considered it, the less he wanted to talk to the cops. No one would believe him, anyway. It all felt so unreal. Perhaps it was best if nobody ever found out. Not even Mel.

Oh yeah? What you gonna do, wander into the flat naked and covered in blood and say, hi honey, I'm home!

"Stop it," he muttered. Even his victorious escape was falling prey to his own self-sabotage. Of course he'd tell his wife and the police what had happened.

Well, probably.

Maybe.

He'd certainly consider it.

Tears sprang to his eyes. "I didn't want to kill her," he said, picturing Myrtle's screaming, tortured face as the shotgun blast destroyed her. "They were going to *kill* me."

The adrenaline was wearing off, and he felt like he was having a heart attack.

You're in shock, he told himself. *Pull over for a minute.*

Pull over? That was ridiculous. Absurd. They were chasing him... weren't they? He hadn't *seen* anyone since he left. But that meant nothing. He glanced in the rearview.

See? Nobody there.

Wait. Was that...? He thought he saw something. A glimpse of light. He pivoted in his seat, peering through the rear window.

No. He was imagining things. With a desperate chuckle, he turned back to face the road.

"Jesus Christ!" he screamed when he saw the hairpin bend dead ahead of him. He slammed the brake. The car skidded, the wheels mounting the verge, kicking up dust and pine cones. A frenzied spin of the wheel, and then the car screeched to a juddering halt inches from a tree trunk.

Dennis sat wide-eyed, his whole body shaking. He gripped the steering wheel so hard his arms hurt.

That had been too close. He coughed, choked, then opened the car door and threw up onto the road, surprised there was anything left inside him. He felt woozy. Delirious. Stabbing pains shot through his chest, and his face and body and feet thrummed in muted agony.

Take a minute. No one's chasing you.

His breaths came in ragged gasps. If he kept driving like this, he was going to lose control of the car, and then everything — the ordeal, the escape — would have been for naught. He checked his feet. They were red-raw and bleeding from dozens of small stones embedded in his skin. He brushed them loose, and levered out the particularly troublesome ones with his fingernails. With each stone he removed, the pains in his chest receded. Gradually, his breathing returned to something approaching normal.

He knew he couldn't manage another five hours like this, but he always kept painkillers in the glove compartment, and—

Shit, his phone!

It lay by the handbrake, the charging cable still plugged into the USB slot. Snatching it up, he saw the missed calls from Mel — forty-seven of them, now — and hit redial. As he waited for her to answer, he opened the glove box and popped two Paracetamol from the blister pack.

"Come on, come on," he said, as the phone rang.

Compulsively, he checked the mirror. He wondered if he'd ever stop checking it.

The road was free of cars. If they were chasing, wouldn't

they have caught up to him by now? Leaning between the seats, he grabbed his overnight bag and emptied it onto the passenger seat. With great difficulty, he slipped on a clean pair of boxers and a tee-shirt. It wasn't much, but it was better than nothing.

The phone kept ringing. "Answer, dammit! Why won't you answer?"

He reached for the keys, but his trembling hands couldn't seem to hold them. He couldn't seem to do much of anything right now, other than sit and shake and cry.

Then, through the open window, he heard it.

The loud blast of a siren.

He looked up at the approaching police car. Through the cracked windscreen, he saw it was slowing.

"Oh god," he muttered, and hung up the phone.

The vehicle pulled over and came to a stop.

Don't panic, don't panic.

Too late.

The officer waited a long time before exiting his vehicle, and when he did, he walked with the unhurried gait of a nature lover enjoying a woodland stroll. Dennis figured it was intentional psychological warfare. The police were probably taught it during training. So, what to do? Should he tell the truth? Or play things cool? Was this cop in on it? Did he know Jenny? Was he *also* married to her?

Too many questions, not enough answers.

The officer arrived at the car. He leaned over and peered in, appraising Dennis's state of undress with a look of bored indifference.

"Good morning," said Dennis. His hands fidgeted on the wheel, and he tried to control them. "Can I help you with anything?" As he spoke, wind whistled through the gaps in his teeth.

The officer — a man, and a good few years younger than Dennis — looked him up and down. "Are you okay?"

What to say to that?

Tell him what happened! He can help you!

"I'm fine, thanks."

The officer stared at him. "You don't look fine."

"I fell."

Brilliant. You fell. What a fucking genius.

"Uh-huh," said the officer.

"Is there a reason you pulled over?"

"I was going to ask you the same thing. This is a dangerous road to stop on. Particularly on a tight corner like this. Then I noticed the dent in the front of your car, and the cracked windscreen, and—"

"I hit a deer," said Dennis, quicker than he wished. "I pulled over to see if it was okay."

"Mm-hmm. And was it?"

"I don't know. I couldn't find it."

"Okay." He nodded slowly. Patronisingly. "So your face is a mess because you fell, and your car is dented because you hit a deer."

"That's right, officer." Dennis cracked a demented smile. "What a day, huh?"

"Indeed." The cop leaned through the window. "So why are you not wearing any trousers?"

He's one of them. He knows.

"Ummm, I always drive like this. That's not illegal, is it?"

"No, I don't believe so." The officer stepped back, his hand resting on his police baton. "Would you mind stepping out of the car, please?"

"Why? I'm sorry I stopped, I just wanted to check on the deer, but now it's gone, I'm gonna—"

"Out of the car, now."

Dennis raised the window and opened the door. Avoiding the puddle of vomit, he winced as he set his bleeding feet on the road. The painkillers had not yet started to work, and he whimpered as he stood.

"What the hell is wrong with your feet?" asked the officer, as a widening pool of blood formed around them.

Dennis shrugged. He was all out of lies. "I... I don't know."

"You don't know?" The officer signalled towards his vehicle. "Follow me, please."

"I really need to get going, officer. My wife is expecting me."

"You're not going anywhere with your feet like that, except to hospital. Come on, I'll drive you."

Dennis's phone rang. At first, the orchestral pomp of The Imperial March was so unexpected that it almost seemed alien, and he stood for a moment, wondering where it was coming from.

"Mel," he said, and leaned into the car to answer. It never occurred to him how suspicious that action might look to a police officer, but then, Dennis wasn't exactly firing on all cylinders.

"Stop right there!" the cop shouted.

Dennis's fingers brushed the warm metal of his phone, and he would have reached it had the officer's groping fingers not snagged the hem of his tee-shirt and hauled him backwards. He swayed into the middle of the road, desperate to keep his balance.

"I need to get that!" he yelled.

The officer slammed the car door shut, and when he reached for his baton, a switch flipped in Dennis's addled brain. He knew it for sure, now. There wasn't a single doubt in his mind.

They were *all* in on it.

"You won't take me back!" he shrieked, and rushed the cop, throwing a wild right hook that connected solidly with the officer's jaw. The cop spun one-eighty from the impact. He faced the Toyota, and Dennis shoved him, watching triumphantly as the officer staggered forwards, slipped in the puddle of vomit, and fell headfirst through the driver's window.

Clenching his fists, Dennis prepared himself for a fight. This wasn't over yet. The tempered glass was designed to shatter into thousands of pieces to prevent long shards from falling onto the vehicle's occupants in the event of a crash. It was a safety feature, and it meant the cop would be relatively unharmed.

Or... or so he had thought.

Yet when the officer hauled his neck free with a soft sucking sound, blood flooded down the car door. And as Darth Vader's theme continued to play, the man turned to him with an expression of unutterable horror.

He was dying, and he knew it.

Dark blood gushed in pulsing waves down the officer's black polo shirt, as several long, wickedly sharp fragments of glass jutted from his torn jugular and gleamed in the dappled sunlight.

"Heeeelllp," the man wheezed. He stumbled two steps to his right, then collapsed, first to his knees, and then onto his side.

"No," said Dennis. His temples pounded. "You're one of them."

The officer lay twitching, his arteries spurting jets of crimson lifeblood across the tarmac. He reached a bloodied hand out to Dennis, who backed away.

"You're in this together. All of you. I know you are!"

Over the moribund officer's indecipherable gurgles and the tinny whine of John Williams's music, he heard tires screeching. A black Land Rover with tinted windows careened around the bend. Dennis shuffled towards his Toyota.

Was it them?

He lurched into the driver's seat. Blood trickled down the inside of the door and pooled in the footrest, and glass cracked beneath his arse as he started the engine. He pulled wildly onto the road, grazing the cop car and knocking the wing mirror off, then slammed his foot down, ignoring the pain that rippled through his tired limbs.

The Land Rover was not slowing. If anything, it sped up as it neared the downed officer, the front wheels bouncing over the prone body, cracking the skull and sending chunks of brain matter arcing through the air. It was them, alright.

Jenny's family had caught up to him.

His phone continued to ring, the looped Imperial March lending an absurd pomp to his life-or-death situation, but Dennis took not his eyes off the road nor his hands from the wheel. The speedometer passed sixty, rushing towards seventy. How fast could his electric-hybrid even go? Not as fast as a four-by-four vehicle specifically designed for rural roads, he wagered.

So if he couldn't outrun them... he would just have to outdrive them.

He pressed his foot down.

The forest shot by like an obscure dream, the road curving madly.

"You won't get me," he muttered. "You'll *never* catch me."

He reached a stretch of relatively straight road and stole a glance in the rearview. The off-road vehicle was closing in. He stabbed the pedal hard. The Toyota hit ninety, the frame vibrating under the pressure. And yet, the needle kept climbing.

According to a speed camera, he had been going fifty-eight miles per hour the night of the crash that had almost ended his life. Ah, but he had been drunk then, and right now, he had never felt so alert, his mind humming on a new, hitherto untapped frequency. A glance at the dial told him the car had passed one-hundred miles per hour.

His phone stopped ringing, and he zoned out, focusing all his attention on the task. A blissful energy descended on him, a zen-like calm that made his nerves tingle and his hairs stand on end. He was losing his pursuers, as the fools slowed for the increasingly perilous curves. Well, he wouldn't stop. Not for the hairpin bends, not for Jenny, not for the cops, not for anyone. He would keep going forever... or at least until he reached his home. They'd never find him. Hell, the only family member that knew his surname was dead, ripped in half by a shotgun blast.

Dennis laughed at the memory.

Careful. Don't lose your head.

The needle hit one-hundred-and-ten. He was really gliding now, time slowing as he navigated the roads like a Formula One champion, the trees a formless mist of browns and greens. There was no trace of the black Land Rover in the mirror.

"I'm gonna make it," he said, and then his phone rang again and he glanced down at the screen. That one simple action — which lasted only a fraction of a second, surely — was enough to break his concentration.

"Mel," he smiled, as he looked back through the wind-screen in time to see he had missed the bend. The car shot up the embankment at almost one-hundred-and-twenty miles per hour. The wheels left the tarmac, and Dennis briefly pondered how fast airplanes had to go before they took flight, before his car hit a tree at an angle and spun, spiralling out of control, smashing hard into another trunk, every window in the car shattering at once in unholy union as the vehicle pitched into the forest and hit the ground in an eardrum rupturing explosion of grinding, broken metal.

And the phone, of course, continued to ring.

11

————

HIS EYES OPENED AS THEY DRAGGED HIM FROM THE CAR.

Somehow, he was still conscious.

He looked up at the bright red sky through the knotted branches of the pine trees. Red?

No, wait.

He chuckled.

That must be all the blood.

Was he dead? He could see, and he could hear... but he couldn't move, and when he tried to speak, all he could do was gargle coppery blood.

"Look," said Jenny. "He's still alive."

"It would be better for everyone if he wasn't," said her father. "Especially for him."

"Ughhhhh," Dennis moaned, and Jenny gazed down at him.

"Don't worry, my love. You're going to be, ummm... okay."

"Aye, you're lucky, son," her father said. "A lot of people would have left you for dead after the shite you pulled. But not us."

Dennis stared up at the man's face.

"Because we look after our own here," the man continued. "And you're part of the family now."

12

As the sun dipped below the trees, Mel Norris switched on the fog lights and wiped the tears from her bleary eyes.

Dennis had been missing for almost twenty-four hours now. She had already spoken to the police, but they were clearly uninterested. Oh, they entertained her concerns, and dutifully took some notes over the phone, but as he was an adult, there was little they could do.

He'll turn up, the woman had said. *He's probably at the pub.*

The words were designed to put her at ease. Instead, she felt sick.

Where *was* he? It was her fault she missed the call. When he rang, she had been in the kitchen making a coffee after a night of fitful slumber. But why hadn't he answered when she phoned back?

Various scenarios played out in her head, each more dreadful than the last. In the most believable one, she imagined him stopping in the pub to use the loo — dammit, why couldn't she remember the name of the place? — and ordering a drink, which then turned into two, then three, and then god knows how many.

He never had known when to stop.

In another scenario, she pictured him hooking up with an attractive young woman, likely an English student impressed by his literary knowledge, and spending the night with her. Again, this was far-fetched. Even at his lowest drunken ebb, Dennis had never cheated on her. It wasn't in his nature. Yet in a curious way, it was the outcome Mel hoped for most. A little infidelity she could forgive, for it was preferable to him picking up the bottle again. And as for the alternatives... that he was missing, or—

"He's okay," she said, as salty teardrops rolled hopelessly down her cheeks. "He's out there, somewhere."

God, she loved that idiot. And since the accident, and his newfound sobriety, she had only grown to love him more.

His addiction, he had told her, began in secondary school. At first, he only drank recreationally, until he discovered alcohol gave him a confidence he otherwise lacked. Soon, he was reliant on booze to get him through social situations, a reliance that swiftly turned to dependence. It got to the point where he would take a shot of tequila before leaving for work or popping to the shops for a loaf of bread.

Thank god he could never afford drugs on a teacher's salary, she thought.

And yet, since that fateful day, things had been going well. They supported each other the way couples should, and had even discussed the possibility of adopting a child. Their love was profound, which was why, without a second thought, Mel had hopped in the car to drive the length of the country in search of her husband, stopping in every roadside lay-by and scanning each parking lot for his car, while watching out for crushed foliage by the side of the road, or a glimpse of wrecked, twisted metal. Her hands trembled as she gripped the wheel.

Why oh *why* had she missed his call?

The tears were really flowing, so she pulled over into a passing place and switched on the hazard lights. There, she rested her head in her hands and sobbed. She called him again, but the phone no longer rang, instead going straight to voicemail. How many tearful messages could one person leave? She pictured him listening to them all, one after the other, a grim catalogue of one woman's mental disintegration.

"Okay, okay, get it together," she sighed, and started the engine. The full beams snapped on, the slender trunks of the pine trees glowing eerily in the glare. Her foot hovered over the pedal, and she was about to drive off when she spotted an object in the middle of the road glinting in the headlights. Something small, something metallic. Something... blue.

My god.

Though she hadn't seen another car since taking the diversion, Mel checked her mirrors for traffic and stepped cautiously out into the night. It was a bracing evening, and she shivered as she walked towards the object, listening for distant engines and ensuring she stayed within the beams of light. She crouched and inspected the broken metal.

A wing mirror.

Her heart leapt into her throat, and then at once, her hopes were dashed. It was *white,* not blue like Dennis's Toyota. The cool glow of the moonlight had tricked her. Mel drew in a long, rattling breath.

"It's not him," she said. "It's not him."

She hugged her jacket tighter. Night was drawing in. Further down the road, she spotted a puddle of dark liquid

— oil, she assumed — but she was more concerned with the tyre tracks that scorched the tarmac as if someone had made a quick getaway.

Could it be him?

She followed the fading tracks past her own vehicle, unsure if she should turn around and head back in their direction. Ah, but Durness — where Dennis's mum had moved in a ridiculous display of independence — was only an hour away. To come this far and not search the last stretch of road would be silly.

Shivering at the biting cold, she climbed back into the car, ready to embark on the final leg of the journey. She would head to Durness, check-in on her mother-in-law, then make the exact same drive in reverse, all while keeping an eye out for the pub Dennis had stopped at.

Rock-something. Or Metal-something. She hadn't been paying full attention because *Doctor Who* was on.

God, her luck was atrocious at the moment.

On she drove through the pine forest, her eyes darting across the road until she came to a small village opposite a field. It was the first glimpse of civilisation she'd encountered in a while, but the lights were all off, the buildings wreathed in darkness. She supposed early nights were typical of farming communities. One thing that *did* bother her was the apparent lack of cars. There were no visible driveways or garages, yet only three vehicles were parked along the road; a rusted Fiat, a Ford Escort, and a black Land Rover. It struck her as unusual for an isolated community to have so few—

Wait.

What was that?

She slammed the brakes, jolting herself into the seatbelt,

and gazed out the window at a large bouquet of flowers propped against a low garden wall.

It looked like a funeral wreath.

With the engine still running, she left the car and walked unsteadily towards the pavement. The flowers were fresh, and arranged around a red postal sack with the Royal Mail logo printed on the side. In the middle was a photo of a grinning man holding a half-finished pint up to the camera. With his bald head and wraparound sunglasses, he looked like the profile picture of every fifty-something man on Facebook.

A cow bellowed in the field, and she sighed. No, the flowers were not in memory of Dennis. Why would they be?

Nobody commemorates the death of a stranger.

Far above, countless stars twinkled in the night sky. As she walked back to her vehicle, music and laughter emanated from a nearby pub on the edge of the village. A drink sounded heavenly right now. Out of solidarity with her husband, she hadn't touched a drop since he quit, but if she wasn't driving, she would happily have ordered a vodka and lemonade in — she squinted — *The Rockarn Inn.*

"Fuck."

A forceful shiver wracked her body.

Was this it? Was this the place?

The Rockarn Inn.

It sounded right. It sounded *better* than right. She hopped in her car and drove the fifty yards to the pub. There were three parking spots, all unoccupied, and she pulled into the closest. Snatching her phone from its dashboard clip, she threw open the door, her heart thumping madly as she selected the photos app and found a good, recent snap of Dennis. The phone slipped from her hands, bounced off her foot, and landed face-up in the gutter.

She knelt to pick the device up, and recoiled. Two white teeth lay on the ground, the roots bloodied as if recently knocked out. What kind of place *was* this? A secret fight club? She picked up her phone — unharmed, thankfully — and headed inside.

A bell tinkled above the door, and she smiled at the few folk who turned to her as she made her way to the bar. They were a surprisingly dapper lot, especially for a Monday evening. The men wore tweed suits, the women frocks and fascinators.

In her pink leggings and baggy sweater with the soup stain on the chest, Mel felt distinctly under-dressed. It didn't matter, she supposed.

She wasn't staying long.

"Excuse me," she said to the barman, raising her voice to be heard over the music.

"What can I get ya?" he asked.

"A lemonade, please." The man looked at her funny — annoyed, even — and she laughed. "Actually, add some vodka to that, if you don't mind."

He broke into a wide grin. "Comin' right up, love."

While he poured the measure and filled the glass, she glanced around the interior. The place was rammed with people, but she couldn't see Dennis.

"There you go," said the barman. "One vodka lemonade." When she produced her wallet, he waved it away. "On the house, tonight."

"Thank you. Can I ask, have you seen this man?" She held up her phone, displaying a picture of her and Dennis at her workmate's wedding. The photo one of her favourites, and a framed copy took pride of place above the living room mantelpiece back home.

The barman studied the photo. "Can't say I have, my love."

"I think he was in here last night. Stopped to use the facilities."

"The what?"

"The toilet."

He chuckled at that. "Nah, I've no' seen him, and I've got a good eye for faces, or so my missus tells me."

Mel sipped her drink. It was strong, and she figured he'd poured her a double measure. "Do you mind if I check with your customers?"

"I dinnae mind, but they might. It's no' a good night for it, I'm sorry to say."

"Oh, really?"

"Aye. We're aw a bit melancholy." He gestured to his left with a subtle nod. "Wee Jenny over there lost her sister this morning."

She followed his gaze to a table in the corner of the room, where a beautiful young lady in a black veil dried her eyes with a tissue. Over the veil she wore a ring of flowers, with an animal skull affixed to it with ribbon.

"God, I'm so sorry to hear that," said Mel. Her heart broke for the woman. She knew how difficult it was to lose a sibling.

"Aye, she's had a tough run of luck, our Jenny."

I know the feeling, thought Mel, though she didn't say so.

"Hard Luck Jenny, some folks round here call her," continued the barman. "Wee lass cannae catch a break."

Mel watched the young woman for a moment, then noticed the figure sitting next to her.

"Jesus," she hissed, her arm jerking involuntarily and knocking her drink across the bar. "Shit, I'm sorry."

The barman smiled knowingly, and used a rag to soak

up the spillage. "Aye, that's her husband. He was in a serious car crash a while back. Jenny and her father found him all crushed up and dying. They had to amputate his legs right there on the side of the road. Can you believe that?"

"That's terrible," said Mel, trying not to stare. She deeply regretted her reaction, but she had been unable to help herself. For it was not the man's lack of limbs that had horrified her, as he sat propped up on a bench with a blanket over his missing legs.

It was his face.

"I know what you're thinking," said the barman, as he furnished her with a replacement drink. "But there wasnae time to take him to a hospital. He was losing too much blood, you see, so they brought him home and patched him up with Jenny's mum's sewing kit. They did the best they could, under the circumstances."

Mel bit her tongue. God bless the two women for saving the man's life, but they had done a *shit* job of his face. The thick slabs of raw meat had been crudely stitched into a patchwork using chunky black embroidery thread. Blood leaked from between the stretched skin, as if the wounds were still fresh.

"When did you say this happened?" asked Mel.

"Oh, y'know. A wee while ago." The barman cleared his throat. "Like I say, she's had a real run of bad luck, our Jenny. But the village always rallies around her in times of need. We look out for each other here. We're like one big happy family."

"That's nice," said Mel, though she was only half-listening. She watched in mounting horror as Jenny held a beer glass up to the round hole that passed for her husband's mouth and tipped it in. He choked, most of the liquid dribbling down his chin, the amber fluid tinted red with blood. "Are you sure he's okay?"

"Aye, he'll be fine. He's got Jenny to look after him. She told me earlier they're trying for a baby, and that she hopes to be with child soon." He grinned. "Look, there she goes now!"

"What the fuck?" breathed Mel, as the young woman stood before her husband and hiked her dress up to her waist. She wore no underwear. Mel didn't know where to look, but like a roadside pileup, she couldn't avert her eyes as Jenny removed the man's blanket, revealing that he, too, was nude. His legs ended above the knees, the stumps wrapped in blood-drenched bandages that dripped steadily over the floor. Jenny took a seat and lifted her husband onto her lap, gripping his exposed buttocks.

"Stop the music!" shouted the barman. "Jenny's trying again!"

A hush fell over the room. People stopped what they were doing and formed a semi-circle around the woman and her husband, shouting and chanting and mercifully blocking the brazen spectacle from Mel's sight.

"That's it!" one of them hollered. "Give 'er the fuck of her life!"

"You can do it!"

"Put it in her!"

The denizens crowded the fornicating couple, clambering over each other to get a better view. One of them started singing.

"Spread her wide, and do the deed,
Put it in, and plant the seed."

Without prompting, the others joined in, forming a ghoulish choir.

"Back and forth, and make her scream,

It's every boy in Rockarn's dream."

Mel glanced around. She was all alone at the bar. A rhythmic clap started up, matching the wet sound of bare flesh smacking against bare flesh, and without a word, she clambered off her stool and walked briskly towards the exit.

"In fae a pound, in fae a penny," the crowd sang, as she slipped unnoticed into the night. *"Aw the laddies love Hard Luck Jenny!"*

"What... the... fuck," she said again, and as a loud cheer erupted from inside, she jogged to her car, got in, and drove the fuck away from The Rockarn Inn, secure in the knowledge that there was no way she'd *ever* find Dennis in a rowdy sleaze-pit like that.

13

THREE YEARS LATER

Dennis, as he so often did these days, was thinking about that night in The Rockarn Inn. When his wife had entered the pub — his real wife, not the insane woman who held him captive — he had known she was there to rescue him. Dear, blessed Mel, come to sweep him up in her arms and carry him from this place of torture and misery. He would have cried, but his tear ducts no longer worked.

Very little of him did.

There he had sat, utterly immobile, desperately trying with every fibre of his being to signal to Mel. And yet, when they finally made eye contact, she had turned away in disgust. Was he so repellant? He didn't know. Since the accident, Jenny had never shown him his face, and kept the bedroom and bathroom mirrors covered by sheets.

His memories of that day were sketchy, but he recalled Jenny and her mother labouring over him from the moment they brought him home. Wide awake, he had lain on the kitchen table as they stabbed embroidery needles into his face, stitching him up. The pain had been excruciating, almost unendurable, and only when they started arguing about whether a particular chunk of meat was part of his cheek or his forehead did he black out.

When he awoke later that evening, Jenny was giving him a light dusting of concealer.

"We're going to be so happy together," she had told him, as she swept the blood-soaked brush across his loose skin. "And don't worry about Myrtle," she added with a cheeky wink. "I never liked her anyway."

Sometimes, at night, he thought about the expression of fascinated horror on Mel's face when she returned her gaze to him. That had been the precise moment his heart — the one thing that still worked — had shattered, for she either didn't recognise him... or didn't care to.

He couldn't blame her.

After all, he had broken his promise and started drinking again. But how else was he supposed to get through the days, trapped in isolation in Jenny's bedroom? Every so often, she would bring home a new husband, at which point her father would wrap him in a blanket and stuff him on top of the wardrobe, where he would lie with his nose pressed to the ceiling, listening to them making love. Those torrid affairs never lasted, though.

"You're my true love, Dennis," she told him one night, as she laid him in the bathtub and hosed him down with the shower. "The rest are just playthings."

Afterwards, she put him to bed and spent ten minutes tightening the threads that held his face together. It was a ritual she performed every few months, as the cords loosened over time, causing his forehead to gradually slide down over his eyes until all he could see was rotten, gangrenous meat.

On nights like this, he preferred it that way, for it meant he was unable to witness the nightmarish atrocities she performed on him, late at night, with that ungodly contraption her father had built for her.

The Arouser, they called it; a narrow, eight-inch-long steel cage with a rounded, bulbous tip like a hollow metal dildo. As Jenny held a bottle of vodka to his smashed lips, letting the liquid gurgle down his throat, he eyeballed the bloodstained machine on the bedside table.

Please... not again. Not tonight.

Jenny screwed the cap back on the bottle and laid it aside.

"It's that time again," she said, and dabbed her sleeve at the dribbles of vodka on his chin. "I'm ovulating. Are you ready to try?"

As if he had a choice.

She casually disrobed, then clambered into bed with him, clutching The Arouser in her clammy hands. Inside the cage, two sharp fishing hooks dangled from thin chains, attached to a series of cogs and gears. The hooks tinkled together mockingly as Jenny placed the cage over his cock and opened a small hatch on the side, through which she carefully pierced the hooks into his foreskin.

"I really feel like tonight's the night," she said, and cranked a wheel on the side of the cage.

Clunk, clunk.

Inside, the chains tightened, stretching his skin taut.

Clunk, clunk.

"Come on lover," Jenny cooed. "Make my dreams come true."

Ah, good old dreams. They were all he had left to occupy

his mind. For the first year of his captivity, Dennis had dreamed of Mel every night. Of holding her tightly, of telling her he loved her, or of simply existing alongside her in their quiet but content way.

Those days, however, were long gone.

Now, he dreamed of one thing, and one thing only; the perfect, agonising release of death.

Clunk, clunk.

Jenny maneuvred herself between his stumps, smearing handfuls of lubricant over the rusted cage in preparation.

"You'll never leave me, will you?" she asked, and although crying was impossible for him now, Dennis had found that, if he concentrated hard enough, he could sometimes force a trickle of blood to seep from one eye socket and roll down his cheek, a simple act that reminded him of what it felt like to weep.

"Do it," Jenny whispered, as she forced him inside her and lay atop his chest. "Make me a baby."

Unable to close his eyes, he simply stared at the pale pink ceiling and waited for it all to be over.

God... he wanted so badly to die.

AFTERWORD

Thank you for reading my anxiety-horror novella Hard Luck Jenny, and I hope you enjoyed it.

The idea for this story came from something that happened to an old friend of mine, a Northern Irish lass who had gone to church for Mass. Upon arrival, she took a seat in the pew and waited for the service to begin. But when it did, she quickly realised she was actually at someone's wake, and found her only escape route blocked by sobbing mourners. Much like Dennis would have done, she ended up awkwardly sitting through the entire service, though unlike our beleaguered protagonist, thankfully she was allowed to leave.

This was over a decade ago, but the story had stuck with me, until one day I decided to write a slightly more 'horror' version, which was actually originally planned as a full-length novel. My outline features an entire *second half* that I completely cut out. In that version, Dennis is forced to go through with the wedding, then spends weeks trapped in the village while Mel searches for him. It was Stephen King's *Misery,* but with a lot of extremely graphic torture and assault and castration, and honestly, I was happy to scrap it. Writing extended torture sequences is no fun, and as much as I enjoy whiplash-inducing tonal changes, the two halves felt totally separate to each other, and honestly, this short version ended up with a much more satisfying ending.

A big thanks to Heather, who I know would drive the length of the country to find me.

Extra special thanks to Boris, who, as I write this, is staring at me without a single thought running through his little domed head.

Kudos to Cheryl for her awesome cover art. Much appreciated!

Cheers to Steve and Connor and Elli, just because.

Shoutout to Maeve for her inspiration.

And thanks to you, dear reader. And might I say, that hat/sweater/shirt/dress* looks really great on you.

*delete as applicable

MUSIC

This entire novella was written to the following three records by German folk-horror band Ivy Chalice, playing on an endless loop:

Noctifer (album)
Dracula (LOTO Book Club Series)
Nachtmahr (Original Score)

EXTRA SPECIAL THANKS TO MY PATRONS

Abbey Lund
Adam Soll
Allie Vanderlaan
Amber Cassady
Anna Crossland
Anna the Cheddar Goblin
Audie Schultz
Brendan & Honey Bunny
Brendan Fitz
Brian Forberger
Britain Gilgour
Brittany Ross
Cameron Roubique
Camille Sara
Carsyn
Cody Phillips
Connor Girvan
Courtney Pearson
Danielle Chiarappa Perkowitz
Dawn Pearson

Destinie

Edward Helton

Elli Wade

Eric Rumsey

Hana Lewis

Hannah Castillo

Hannah Orr

James Hill

Jarrod Linehan

Jeb Caffee

Joctan Hernandez

Joe Brewer

Josh Heaps

Joshua Carter

Kate H

KD Davies

Kevin Kelly

Kim DeCillo

Landyn Tedrick

L.J. Dougherty

Luke Martin

Matt Mccleland

Matthew House

Mel Kaye

Meredith Jensen

Michelle S

Mike McDougal

Newton Webb

Nicola Swordy

Nicole Stephens

Noah Andruss

Patricia Palacios

Peter Jilmstad

Extra Special Thanks to my Patrons

Phoebe Thompson
Phillipillar
Phil Otter
Rebecca Vale
Rob Jeromson
Robert L
Roberto Hull
Rochelle Hennings
Ryan Orgel
Sarah Brown
Sebastian Ersson
Steve Stred
Susanne Bouwmeister
Tyler Geis
Vickie Allan
Vivian

ABOUT THE AUTHOR

David Sodergren lives in Scotland with his wife Heather and his best friend, Boris the Pug.

Growing up, he was the kind of kid who collected rubber skeletons and lived for horror movies. Not much has changed since then.

His best known books include the gory and romantic fairy tale The Haar, the blood-drenched folk-horror Maggie's Grave, and the analog-horror fever dream Rotten Tommy. David also writes under the pseudonym Carl John Lee, publishing splatterpunk novels such as Psychic Teenage Bloodbath and Cannibal Vengeance.

instagram.com/paperbacksandpugs

ALSO BY DAVID SODERGREN

The Forgotten Island

Night Shoot

Dead Girl Blues

Maggie's Grave

The Navajo Nightmare (with Steve Stred)

The Perfect Victim

Satan's Burnouts Must Die!

The Haar

And By God's Hand You Shall Die

Rotten Tommy

Summer of the Monsters

Death Spell

Writing as Carl John Lee

The Blood Beast Mutations

Horror House of Perversion

Cannibal Vengeance

Horror House of Perversion 2: The Slaughtered Lambs

Psychic Teenage Bloodbath

Death Freaks on Hell's Highway

Psychic Teenage Bloodbath II